novum pro

Carys Smith

A Little Less than Love?

novum pro

www.novum-publishing.co.uk

Printed in the European Union on environmentally friendly, chlorine- and acid-free paper.

ISBN 978-3-99064-158-3
Editing: Julie Hoyle, B.Ed (Hons)
Cover photo:
Pretoperola | Dreamstime.com
Cover design, layout & typesetting:
novum publishing

www.novum-publishing.co.uk

Prologue

"All sorrows can be borne if you put them into a story ..."
Isak Dinsen

PRESENT DAY

"How was I to know you would come along and fu.k my life up?"
Scream 2014

That box had not seemed so difficult when it was put into the loft: a stretch on the chair, a quick shove. Getting it down though was turning out to be a different experience. Just bringing in the step ladder and taking those up fourteen measly stairs had been hard going. By the fourth stair she had to drag, rather than carry it up and by the last she found herself sitting down for five minutes to catch her breath. How stealthily one gets old: and now there was the prospect of a shaky ascent and the even shakier reaching up to negotiate.

At last she was on the top step and determinedly willed her knees to remain steady. The box was only a few inches from the edge but still, maybe a reach too far. Perhaps she should wait for Keith? His six-foot frame and long arms would have no trouble. For him it was just a puny cardboard box.

Although only a couple of feet long and maybe a foot high, the box was an awkward bulky shape without convenient cut out hand grips. Up close, she could see that little sharp mouse teeth had been feasting on it. Was that a distinct smell of rodent wafting from the open hatch? Maybe everything inside had been eaten, or could there be a snug nest full of baby mice she would disturb?

Was it worth it? Was it worth what suddenly seemed like a two-way risk to bring down that box? She paused and forced herself to consider the very serious question of whether she really wanted or needed to release a forgotten part of her life, conveniently shut away in the dark, for nearly two decades.

Her classical days and a grim tale of a box being opened sprang to mind. It was really a jar – but box or jar, the point was, that Pandora opened it and unwittingly released all the evils into the world.

The Past

Diary Entry

She in a bright blue dress,
stood in the doorway.
A flash of white in dark hair,
pleasantly asking a question.
I cracked a casual joke but
must confess, as the door closed,
I was seriously smitten!

Eve looked up and said, with (well I think so) a bit of a smug smile, "Do you know who that is?"
"No. Should I?" I said, pretending to be only mildly curious.
"That's Dian Wilson, our new boss!"

Seriously! Oh crap!

Part One

A Little Less than Love?

CHAPTER ONE

The Past

Grace

As Grace left with the dog she studiously avoided the distinctive single envelope that lay on the mat. The red-blue of its stripe plainly stating it must be from America and the extreme sloping right hand also plainly stating it was from Dian.

Once upon a time she would have picked it up in pleased anticipation and called out its arrival to Lecce. Once upon a time they would have read it together at the breakfast table and discussed their mutual friend's luck in having the freedom to enjoy yet another exciting holiday destination. The jokes and quips inside would have been meant for the both of them: once upon a time.

Grace hurried out and away from it, whistling for Ruby to follow, doggie bags in one hand and the lead in the other. Quickly she crossed the road and made for the park, hardly slowing to allow for Ruby's quota of sniffs and stops.

For a while she distractedly threw the ball and paced the large grassy circle until she gave up and slumped down onto the bench and considered the envelope and its unwelcome arrival into their lives. Should she ignore it, leave it where it was until Lecce found it when she left for work. Should she put it next to her cereal bowl, propped up against the tea pot as if nothing was out of the ordinary?

It was late November, the day was bright but cold, Grace shivered as she stood, zipping up her jacket and calling to Ruby who was busy investigating the overgrown shrubby area with a small terrier and an ancient Labrador. This was their morning routine; throw the ball, walk the circle, let Ruby investigate the shrubs with her friends, wave to Howard from two doors down and hurry home to Lecce and breakfast. A sharp stab of loss pierced as she imagined how the world might look without the happy and contented certainty of their together-forever life.

Grace took her time walking home continuing to worry over the possible significance of the sudden silences that had grown between them recently. Was Lecce still as happy and contented as she, and if not, why hadn't she said anything. Was Dian still only their much loved mutual friend? How could over a decade of easy-going communication have dissolved so imperceptibly into dangerous no-go areas she was unwilling to cross; afraid to bring out into the open?

Reaching their door she delayed a few moments longer, taking off her gloves, unclipping Ruby's lead and fishing in her cluttered pocket for the key, suddenly reluctant to step through and see whether the letter had remained where she had left it, was open on the table for her to read, or spirited away without a word.

Diary Entry

There was an airmail letter from Dian this morning. It was addressed to me. I was more than surprised. I was excited, overwhelmed and guilty. I stuffed it in my work bag and rushed off early. I must have read it a hundred thousand times but, as usual; I don't know what she means. She's on holiday with her husband but would rather sit next to me? I bet he wouldn't be a bit impressed! What is she really thinking? What does she want?

Oh! I adore that woman (unfortunately!)

Excerpt from Letter

Harvard Yard
Mass.
I thought of you all the way up the M4 – all the fields had blond crew cuts – but these had wood pigeons nitpicking! I also thought of you all the way to America. If we had been together, what laughs and jolly japes! That thought was so strong I felt almost willing to perch on the boniest knee of the oldest pensioner if the airline would only put me on a return flight! Of course, preconditioning (common sense?) kicked in and ***I did no such thing. Would do no such thing!***

CHAPTER TWO

The Past

Lecce & Dian

When Lecce had bought the cards she had thought of them as a bit of a joke or a half joke anyway. When she had posted them she told herself the same thing. It was all part and parcel of their flirty friendship and meant no more, and no less. At the same time she had chosen a particularly overly sentimental and expensive one for Grace.

As she stood on the doorstep poised ready to rap on the brass knocker of Dian's town-house a vague self-loathing swept dimly across her conscience, almost squashing the excited anticipation she had experienced all morning since the call. Grace's face had not shown pleasure at the card but had registered a subtle glimpse of hurt before she had smiled her thanks and handed across a beautifully self-painted portrait of two love birds inside a heart with their phrase: *together-forever* carefully inscribed in gold pen beneath.

She glanced up at the second floor window and back across to the safety of her car. There was still time to leave, to rush back to work and call Dian with an excuse. Irresolute, she had quietly lowered the knocker and half turned before she heard the sharp tap of heels on tiles and the swing of a heavy door being opened.

"Welcome!" Dian took her hands and air kissed both her cheeks, "I was listening out for you – and here you are – how lovely!"

Lecce mutely followed Dian up the two flights, ridiculously in awe of candy stripped regency wallpaper and the ornate banister. This was her first invitation to the place Dian had always described as her "pied-a-terre" that only the "favoured few may enter." She had a sudden longing for her own homely two by two, terraced cosily between Barbara on the one side and old Arthur and Nesta on the other.

The apartment door was already open. Lecce had an unexpected glimpse of their reflections in a long elegant dress mirror that stood just inside on the left. For some obscure reason her eye was drawn down to their feet; her trainers, Dian's court shoes. It was this incongruous difference in footwear that made her wonder, not for the first time, what she and this stylish, sophisticated, much older and much married woman, thought they were doing: this place, this woman, were so out of her league!

Diary Entry

Oh dear! Dian and her house are so grand – and oh dear! I am so common.

I'm sure she almost kissed me in the hallway. Unprepared I did an embarrassing bunny-hop back step. In the dining room were those old-fashioned Babycham glasses with fake pink champagne and glace cherries on sticks. We chinked glasses and again she went to kiss me but I was already knocking back the pseudo-champagne as if it were the real thing! (***plank***).

A bit later we began a rock n roll dance to Roy Orbison on an incredibly worn, but handsome Persian rug. We danced so naturally, so in sync, but all too soon it was interrupted by the telephone. It was Rose asking me to come back to work as the Greek 0-level parents were wreaking havoc outside the exam room again!

As I reluctantly left, she handed me a lovely card with two women on the front cover and inside, a touching poem where she had added: "*She holds the woman in the flowered robe like an Oscar newly-won.*"

Oh I adore that woman ... what am I going to do?

The Past

Excerpt from Letter

Nirja
Spain

My star! My love! My joy!
You are the thin blue line; the silver between the sky and the sea! I could weep to leave you so soon after just a few loving nights.
Alas, married duty calls, and we are here in Nerja for the next ten days. Be sure I carried you in my heart (ah, if only in my luggage!). And be sure that I will write, and write and write and try and phone when prudent. Soon I will have shredded the calendar and will fly home to you on B.A.'s wing ..ed chariot!
Meanwhile, here is the key to my hearth and house. Make yourself as much at home there as you already are in my heart.
Dx
P.S. The longest nights are those without you.

Diary Entry

What a love letter! It was tucked inside a very striking note card by someone called Georgia O'Keeffe. I looked her up and apparently, her flower paintings are really erotic art! Well, it just looks like a rather beautiful painting of a flower to me! Anyway, I love that letter.

It feels so strange, after three whole years of wishing to have my prize. My newly-won Oscar! Such a romantic letter is a far-cry from the almost business-like dinner at her place last Wednesday (will I ***ever*** forget!) I don't remember discussing the terms and conditions of an affair before! Looks like she's still the boss! Do all married women broker deals before they get into bed?

That doesn't mean it wasn't romantic! Oh, it was! We had finished our dinner and were sitting in her window seat, our knees just touching. It was already dark and the bare bones of all those tall, neatly spaced street trees were rather ghostly silhouettes under the lamp lights. It is such an old, quiet street that I wouldn't have been a bit surprised if a coach and four had suddenly trotted out of the foggy gloom, lantern swinging, like something out of Dickens!

We were both rather self-conscious, I think, and we were mostly silent. I could hear the clock in her hall tick in time to my pulse (or so it felt!). At last she took my hands and said very seriously, "Your poem seemed to hint that you would like me to kiss you. Shall I kiss you?"

It was only then that I realised that for all our friendship and flirting, I hardly knew this rather handsome and glamorous older woman. Left to me, I think I would have hesitated forever, and we would be sitting there even now!

How strange and enchanting it is to be kissed and kiss for the first time. I never thought about it before, but ***it is*** rather like an act of faith, of truth, or an oath perhaps: a hope that these lips and your lips will always be kind. It was such a deep and long and lovely kiss and of course everything else was easy after that.

Would Dian mind if I write that her breasts are the most youthful and beautiful I have probably ever had the privilege to see and yes, to touch? I heard myself exclaim, "Oh, they are just lovely, how lovely they are!" And she laughed, and replied, rather proudly, "Yes, they aren't bad now let's take off ***your*** shirt!"

Oh dear! This is just my old diary but I dare not write anymore, I mustn't kiss and tell, but what a sexy lady! Surely it can't be "wedded bliss" that has made her so enthusiastic, joyful and fun! Wouldn't it be wonderful if it ***was me!***

Later I asked her why she had never left her husband officially and she said, "Because he doesn't deserve it." Well if someone doesn't make you happy, and you prefer to live on your own for more than half the week, doesn't that mean they do deserve it? But I didn't say that, did I? No, of course not! I just wanted more kissing and more of everything else and to forget there was anything complicated coming our way!

But of course, there is, and it will! After all, she is on holiday with her ***husband.*** And I shall have to talk to Grace as soon as she's back from London. Well, like Scarlet O'Hara, "I'll think about ***that*** tomorrow".

CHAPTER THREE

The Past

GRACE

Grace never understood why it was always here, in this uninspiring substation that the Paddington to Cardiff always chose to interrupt its journey. For a moment the train stood stationary but optimistic, still chugging noisily, before the squealing brakes shut down completely and hissed into a silent halt.

She looked up from her magazine and out at the familiar untidy and dispirited hedgerows just behind the wire fencing. The moody February sky with its grey looming clouds threatened rain, lots of it: or perhaps sleet. It was cold enough. Even without this stop there was over two hours to go and by the time she arrived it would be dark.

Momentarily, this station, this tedious journey, this weather, threatened to overwhelm. She had longed for and dreaded her return; from the moment she had boarded the train to London, during the long days with Maeve and Bobby who had valiantly tried everything to lift her mood and since Lecce had finally called this morning.

Her promise to cook a vegetarian lasagne had not reassured. Instead it brought to mind the fleeting bitter pain of the extravagant valentine's card and now the possible reason behind this gesture. The old Lecce would have hopped across to the Chinese takeaway and picked up a supermarket bottle of red. That was the Lecce she wanted to go home to.

The ticket collector had asked twice before Grace registered his presence at her elbow. Numbly, and with a polite watery smile, she handed over her ticket before slipping it back into her wallet. She tried not to picture the photograph she always kept inside: Ruby red dog with the three cats underneath her protective and sagging stomach, the irrepressible beauty of their June garden and Lecce sprawled and grinning like a Cheshire cat on their faded and tatty garden furniture.

Only now, at long last, could they afford new furniture and even the barbeque Lecce had always pined for. They could have a long summer holiday somewhere hot, or a walking tour in Lake Garda. A stab of frustration and fear clutched at her heart and squeezed. Why now, when everything was looking so good was Lecce doing this to them?

Finally the train started up with a judder and began a slow crawl away from the station. As the engine picked up speed in earnest Grace thought perhaps it would be better if she stayed stranded and stalled in Didcot Parkway forever. She did not want to hear what she knew Lecce would have to say. Lecce, her Lecce, was no good at secrets, or lies, she would want to make a clean breast of it and find the kind of impossible compromise that just did not exist.

With a deep painful thud inside she thought of Dian. If only she could hate her with the kind of scorching jealousy she deserved: but she was too nice and too patently vulnerable for that. She brushed at her eyelids. Dian would never leave her husband and Lecce would soon tire of being a weekday mistress: if that was what she had already become.

Lecce and Grace

The animals were the first to hear Grace arrive. They ran rejoicing as a pack, to the front door, Ruby barking, the cats bristling with pleasure. Lecce joined them, hurriedly closing the kitchen on all its mess. Grace was truly soaked. Why would she never take a taxi, or at least an umbrella?

Lecce was conscious of fussing in the way she used to with the children. Dabbing Ineffectually at the wet shoulder length hair with her tea towel; until she felt Grace stiffen and move away.

Both women were only a little over five feet and for a brief moment their eyes met on the level and held until Lecce dropped her own, backing off in guilty confusion, babbling about her lacklustre efforts with dinner. Grace knew, that was obvious, and it was awful but also a relief. She was no good with secrets and always unsuccessful with lies.

"Well, you get yourself together and I'll try to make sense of that blessed lasagne," she said with a small contrite smile, "I'll put the kettle on. You must be cold."

For a while they managed small talk, pushing the burnt crispy topping of the meal to one side, neither eating much, both waiting for the other. Finally Lecce looked across at Grace, at the sweet face she knew so well but never tired of; the round blue eyes, the small button nose, and those endearing flat ears behind which her rarely combed hair was invariably tucked.

Grace set down her fork and folded her hands into her lap, head slightly to one side, her expression attentive. It was a pose that Lecce, shamefaced, recognised as the one she used with her clients, kind but vaguely impersonal, giving every appearance of a non-judgemental objectivity. Grace rarely shouted, hardly ever lost her temper and, Lecce thought hopefully, always forgave.

"I'm sorry, so very sorry Grace but I … but I …"Lecce grappled with the week- long confusion of her thoughts and continued in a rush, " … it's just … I just couldn't resist … I know how stupid it is but I just couldn't, can't help myself."

There was a long silence, so long, that Lecce became afraid that Grace would never answer, that she would be forced to find some other explanation, or to promise what she already knew she could not.

"No, it's not that stupid," Grace said finally with a shrug, "I can understand how charismatic and attractive Dian must seem to you, and how flattered you must feel," she paused before adding, her voice rising ," but what is stupid is for you to believe for one second that she will ever leave her husband. And what is more stupid is that you would give up all of this."

She swept out an angry arm which seemed to encompass not just the room but their entire lives together; the piecemeal furniture they had painstakingly collected, the framed portraits of the children in different stages of growth and the animals that sat silent and staring at them in perplexity.

"For what – just sex or what … what … what!"

"I don't know. I was married once," Lecce faltered.

Grace's tone of sudden vehemence surprised them both. It was accompanied by a dark red mottled flush that quickly began to cover her face and neck.

Even before Grace had jumped up, had pushed her half full plate onto the floor, and had run from the room screaming in panic,

"I don't know what to do! I don't know what to do! Tell me what to do!"

Lecce had grown more than a little afraid of where this might lead them. She sat staring down at her own inedible dinner and began to count the cost. How had she ever imagined that this could be negotiated into some kind of open relationship; see where it leads scenario without consequences or loss to either of them? To all of them: the children, her parents, the animals, and their happy home together.

Lecce realised with a sad certainty that this decade of blessed calm and tranquilly that Grace had gifted her had been smashed to pieces along with the plate and the contents that lay dripping and staining the new carpet, and it was all a mess entirely of her own making.

Yet, although her own heart was just as cracked, her own mind a fearful jumble of loss and confusion, she also had enough self-knowledge to realise that she was compelled to blunder on, unable to prevent her uncontrollable urge to rush into whatever chaos awaited and back to the arms of Dian.

Diary Entry

When Grace ran from the room I just didn't know what to do either. So I ran out to Spar and bought a bottle of Merlot. After a couple of glasses she calmed down, we both sat and cried, for ages and ages. Later we crawled into the same bed and just lay there holding hands, flanked by the animals, who were sitting around in the open doorway like sentinels trying to prevent an impending doom!

The animals hated it and stood staring at us, (at me probably), cats pressed close to Ruby, wide eyed, their fur puffed and spiky.

This isn't what I had meant to happen. What had I thought would happen? Oh, something much more impossibly easy and sophisticated I expect!

Mum and Dad are bewildered and I haven't dared tell the kids. I haven't even told Dian. She will be mortified, and want us all to talk about it, or throw me over straight away.

And now I have recorded my folly. I longed for romance, I longed for Dian, but getting what you long for can be pretty shitty for other people.

CHAPTER FOUR

Present Day

Lecce

It was still far too cold to spend long hours in the allotment. Why did Eliot insist that April is the cruellest month? This drab February had delivered nothing but unending rain, ceaseless wind and a bone-penetrating chill.

It was two o'clock: a quiet time. There was a soothing absence from the usual vigorous activity that generally included whining strimmers and the deeper growl of rotavators. The hammering and the sawing had been quieted by the cold and darkness of the day. There was no other sound but far off traffic and birdsong. She decided it was most likely the ever optimistic blackbird.

Lecce peered through the rain-streaked greenhouse windows. The lid of the bonfire bin had blown off again. She noticed how old it had become. One of the legs was missing and the whole thing was listing precariously; yet its red rust was oddly pleasing on such a colourless afternoon. Through the open door she caught the faint whiff of wood smoke and wondered if she should have a final farewell bonfire before replacing it with one of those new shiny metal ones with the smart chimney.

God knows it would be a good idea to burn that wretched diary. The first few of the entries had left her puzzled and uncomfortable. They seemed to carry an air of foreboding in their blue-lined pages. The tightly cramped writing was hardly recognisable as her own rounded, even hand.

It would be hard to burn those early letters though. Full of purple prose from one and something far more in your face from the other! Suddenly her heart was suffused with elated warmth. To have once been so loved, so admired, by two such very different and attractive women! How gratifying and amazingly incredible. Really, she knew herself to be only human, not "wonderful" or "shining" and not particularly "sexy".

The sweet song of the blackbird stopped abruptly as did that warmth which was quickly replaced by a vague premonition that much of what followed was definitely not so wonderful or shining. What else was inside? Were there other letters other memories that would be painful if revealed? Why had she deliberately packed them away and left them out of sight and out of mind for so long?

★★★

The following afternoon Lecce decided to delay the read or burn decision and spend some time at the local gym instead. It was a new routine and one that had taken a big leap of faith. These days though, just getting into her training kit seemed to drop twenty years off. Maybe retirement was the new middle age!

She need not have worried that she would feel the outsider. Plenty of people of her generation were to be seen lifting weights, tackling rowing machines or simply just running and cycling as she did. This new obsession was not only giving her back a waistline but had also returned a former love: popular music.

When had she stopped listening to modern pop? It had always been such a permanent backdrop to her life, especially of her romantic life. As she tugged on her special sports socks and hi-tech trainers, she fumbled with this thought. A brief replay, like an old black and white newsreel, gave her a fleeting fragment of a familiar song in a car; a glimpse of two people pressed together in a passionate embrace, an almost taste of an urgent kiss on her lips.

Her mind resolutely pulled away from that hazy image. That was then: now her iPod was just an integral part of her workout. Those young men and women, their plaintive songs of confusing betrayals and loss were, thankfully, ***their*** Greek tragedy chorus. Or were they?

As Lecce sat in the over-heated changing room, swallowing a bottle of water and preparing herself for vigorous exercise, she wondered vaguely why she had avoided the prospects of a new romance. Any passing interest on her part or the occasional overtures from others had been quickly repulsed. Somehow, she had become wary of listening to music and even more wary of involving herself with a stranger offering more than casual friendship.

Lecce stood up briskly, switching on her music, drowning out those uncomfortable thoughts. That muddle in the box; those postcards, poems and any other joyless insights were disturbing her carefully ordered life. It was better to burn the lot in her new bin: maybe tomorrow?

CHAPTER FIVE

The Past

DIARY ENTRY

Your court shoes
my trainers.
Are we walking a tandem
two-step?
Or am I just a weekday
Mistress
and you a weekend wife?

Mum said, "Your Dian is a lovely woman. Is there any chance she'll leave her husband?"
I was still annoyed that she'd rushed out to "introduce herself" so I just shrugged and told the truth, "I've no idea."

★★★

THE PAST
DIAN AND LECCE

(one year later).

Dian's wide smile of welcome slowly faded replaced by a moment's confused panic she was unable to disguise.

"Well, are you going to invite me in?" Lecce said her own smile fading into one of amused surprise, adding when Dian remained as if rooted to the spot, "Baby, it's cold out here."

"Come on in sweetie," Dian moved quickly aside and searched for her customary good manners, "I was just a bit surprised to see you all dressed up in your … in your …" she trailed off and gestured at the dress mirror and the likeness of Lecce who continued to stand, with growing discomfort on the threshold.

Lecce took a tentative step forward turned to the mirror and examined her reflection, oddly transposed behind Dian's own. Dian was wearing her favourite blue dress which picked up the exact shade of her eyes. Her hair, newly styled, had a silver white sheen under the dim hallway lighting. As always, she looked absolutely gorgeous and, Lecce had never noticed before: very, very … straight!

As for herself, she saw more or less what she expected to see; a woman not yet far into middle- age, short in stature, sportive and compact in build with a mop of blond highlighted hair. She had on a new, crisp white dress shirt that hid pink elephants behind the jacket and a red bowtie borrowed from her father. She gave a sharp laugh of vague recognition.

"Ah … is it the bow tie that makes me look so … so … gay! Mum said you might think it a bit much!"

There was a long strangled silence before Dian, still flustered, stepped into the kitchen and turned her back to fill the kettle.

"I just think that maybe it's all a bit too … too … you know … making too much of a statement, especially tonight being … being …"

Lecce left the mirror and followed her into the kitchen and said carefully, pushing away the quick darts of indignant anger that threatened to surface, "Are you ashamed of me … ashamed of us?"

"Of course not, but perhaps Valentine's Night is not the night to ... well parade our difference?" Dian turned and kissed her briefly. "Darling, you look wonderful, magnificent, but you know that I need to be discreet ... that I just can't ... that I don't actually want to be ... to be ..." she frantically grappled for the right words, "noticed like that."

Lecce stepped back and without reply walked into the bedroom where she opened the carrier bag her mother had pushed into the passenger seat just as she was leaving.

"You look lovely dear, really stunning." Her mother had said, "but take this though, just in case."

Lecce inspected the dreadful apricot jumper her Aunt Jean had given her for Christmas and realised two things: this was a straight alternative and her mother understood Dian in a way she never would.

Diary Entry

I changed into the hideous apricot 1980's throwback, wondering all the while why how I was dressed mattered, tonight, of all nights; our anniversary of our almost Valentine's night a year ago.

The restaurant was disappointing and shabbier than I remembered. The tablecloths were made of paper and the flower on the table was plastic. The place was practically empty and there wasn't even any background music. Usually, we would have found it all highly amusing and Dian would be making whispered comments in a fake Italian accent. Yet we sat silent and glum for the most part. I can't remember if the food was decent or not. I couldn't taste a thing. The waiter made it worse by saying,

"Have dessert ladies. After all, it is Valentine's night!"

My disguise and her masquerade didn't do such a good hetero job then! Perhaps we should have stayed in and got a take away? What does my Mum know about Dian that I don't?

Later, we tried to discuss it rationally but I was still too grumpy about her going off to Paris last weekend with that husband of hers. They must be far more connected than I had imagined. How does going off to Paris together relate to a weekend arrangement of convenience?

I ended up shouting about women who want to screw other women but still like to hide behind their straight credentials! I might've added something stupid about married-looking dresses and court shoes too. (Oh yes, and handbags!)

"I'm not a lesbian!" she yelled back.

"What are you then?"

"I'm just me! I'm just me, or bisexual," and after a long pause, "maybe."

For some reason that made us laugh fit to bust and exhausted, we called a truce.

Later, as we were getting ready for bed, I asked, "Don't you feel like you're in chains?"

And she said, "No, sweetie. The only true chains are the chains of love. And I do so love you!"

How charming! How could I resist? We made up, of course. We made love for hours and hours. Our bodies just melted together like two halves: as if we were dancing a two-step in complete harmony. Even when we eventually slept, we woke at the very same moment and began kissing whilst still half asleep. It was the strangest Valentine's night ever – horrible and wonderful!

I suppose that's make up sex, then? Yet, we didn't solve anything.
But I still adore that woman!
Oh, I hope I do.

CHAPTER SIX

Lecce

Present Day

Lecce was in her favourite room. The conservatory, with its south-facing aspect and wide picture windows, was light and airy. Even on the gloomiest day it was impossible to feel cooped up inside, especially when the indoor plants bloomed and there was the luscious fragrance of bougainvillea and lemon blossom in the air.

This chaotic order of casually stored garden paraphernalia was her true escape: her dream space. Here all her seasonal planning was done; her cuttings propagated and her seeds sown. Every changing season was marked by a new list of optimistic notes scribbled on a large old whiteboard, rescued from the college skip.

As she remembered Billy's caustic remarks about the point of skips being to throw things away, she realised with surprise that her working life was already five years into history. It was strange how many people and events still lived so vividly in the back of her mind. And stranger still, that the box and its contents, that part of her life, was such a blank. Apart from the rash of muddled dreams that had begun almost as soon as it had come down.

Recently, the large and battered workbench with the board propped in the middle had taken on a new focus. The box was placed on the left and most of its contents were now stacked in a variety of differently shaped piles to the right. As each bundle grew, Lecce was sure that the key to the reason for her search would suddenly materialise. A camera- eye would click open on her wilful amnesia: the blind reaching out for a vital clue just beyond her grasp would be over in an instant.

So far, she had not liked all that she had learned about that younger Lecce: those rash, hurtful acts of betrayal. All born from a selfish desire she had believed could not be denied. Yet her older self retained a grudging empathy for that still young woman with a heart on her sleeve who had somehow retained an optimistic belief in lasting romantic love.

With an effort she brought herself back to the collection of papers and picked up all those with the familiar NHS insignia. Lecce could think of no good reason why she would have kept these. The fistful of papers remained briefly poised on the edge of the recycle bag before she pulled back and begun to leaf through each one with care, a slight frown creasing between her eyes.

Although each letter was unremarkable on its own, she suddenly recalled how quickly they had seemed to stack up with an alarming regularity. How irritated she had become with the way they had constantly disrupted her working life and had curtailed even the least risk-taking of her sporting activities.

Lecce felt a sudden stab of remorse as she thought of how easily resentful she had been every time Dian's other life had taken precedence, leaving her to look for other company at her appointments or surgeries.

Obviously, what she had expected had not been what she had been promised. Hindsight was such a wonderful, frustrating thing. Dian had been completely open and definite about her priorities in the beginning; there was an elderly father, a frail mother in law, a husband and numerous other commitments.

Why had she expected the unquestioning and undivided support Grace and she had shared? How had she so easily, so casually, parked Grace and their fulfilling life together in an isolated corner of her thoughts? Her children – their children – had been far more caring and constant. That box was certainly providing a glaring spotlight on her selfish side. And then, there was the inevitable disenchantment with Dian's unwillingness to commit to more than a secret affair. Yet, surely, it would have taken far more than those mistakes and disappointments for her to become a romantic recluse for two decades? To almost completely forget what must have been a huge turning point in her life.

A sickening rising panic and an unexpected glimpse of malevolence somewhere in her mind's eye left her powerless to turn away. A slender, shadowy figure unexpectedly crystallised and hovered in between her conscious and unconscious memory. A fluttery fear-bird sensation began a frenetic thrash inside as her heart lurched in an unnervingly familiar way.

With an effort Lecce pulled away from the table, thrusting the sheaf of appointment letters into the recycling. She backed through the alcove, unsteadily reaching behind her in a desperate search for the solid wooden arms of the corner chair.

For long moments she sat quite still, filling her mind with no more than the quiet tick of the clock and the indistinct murmur from the radio. Eventually her rapid breathing calmed but she remained rooted to the seat edge of the chair until she was quite certain that every faint trace of that indistinct ghost had receded back into her un-remembering mind.

CHAPTER SEVEN

The Past

Postcard

My darling girl!
How far away you seem and how many times a day do I wish you were here with me? Too many, far, far too many! We could be admiring the beach huts and eating the sticks of stripy rock I know you so love. My rock would have your name all through it. And yes! I could eat you up! There are many cottages with roses around the door. Some whose toes (if cottages had toes!) would touch the sea when it comes in! And how lovely that would be! For you and for me!
Home soon and goodbye to Sir for a few precious days!
Dx

Diary Entry

I got a postcard from Dian today addressed to Mistress Lecce! She meant it as a joke, I know. But I can't see the funny side. I don't like the way she always calls her husband "Sir" either.

When she comes home I'm going to tell her but I bet she'll just say, like she always does, "I'm just playing the game sweetie." Or I'm such a "delicious secret."

So: there are a lot of words I'm beginning not to like: mistress, sir, game and secret.

What about delicious?

Oh dear, I don't know anymore, I just don't know.

★★★

Lecce and Dian

Still half asleep Lecce made an instinctive grab at the telephone. Its shrill cry had jolted her awake completely, dispelling the remnants of a happy dream, now impossible to recall. Until she heard Dian's thundering feet across the landing she was still only semi-conscious and the injunction to never-ever pick up the phone was forgotten. She snapped her mouth shut just in time and apologetically held out the handset towards Dian who took it with a restrained polite snatch.

At first Lecce thought it must be the dreaded "sir." She scrutinised Dian's face, which had coloured and then abruptly paled and appraised the tone that had begun politely brisk but had then quickly softened. Slowly it dawned on Lecce that her continued presence in the room was intrusive. The call was not only unexpected but also intensely personal.

The voice, clear enough through the mouthpiece, identified as an unknown male. Carefully she edged out of bed and made for the bathroom, shutting the door quietly behind her, fighting the urge to lean against it and eavesdrop. Instead she showered long and noisily, taking her time finding her clothes in the spare room and putting on the scanty makeup she always felt obliged to wear at work.

Their breakfast table usually so relaxed and cheering to them both, had quickly grown oppressively thick with Lecce's unspoken suspicions and Dian's continued discomposure. Their continued silence seemed to amplify every chink from a plate or spoon, the pouring of tea became a rushing torrent into the cup. Lecce sat with eyes downcast, swallowing down the urge to press for an explanation, her lips tight with effort.

"In case you're wondering," Dian said eventually, "that was just an old, old friend I haven't heard from for the longest time." She busied herself buttering toast and pouring more tea, just a slight tremble of her hand betraying any anxiety. Why had Andrew called and why this morning? What had he heard? "Well, more of an old flame really, someone I never thought to hear from again."

Lecce felt herself colour and the uncomfortable sensation of a hot jealous pang which immediately transmuted into a sharp stab of pain behind her right eye. She knew that Dian had had other affairs throughout her thirty years of marriage all were with men, she had supposed. This must be one of them.

"I suppose you're going to see him," she said, "even if he hasn't bothered to get in touch for the longest time," she was unable to resist the sarcasm that bit at her tongue and the indignation that flared and continued to flush her face.

Dian put down her cup and looked warily across at her lover, resolving to be honest. Lecce was always so un-accepting of lies, and would not forgive if found out later, "I don't know sweetie, it's taken me by surprise and I'm going to have to think about it," unconsciously she twisted the rings on her marriage finger, "but whatever I decide, it doesn't have to change things between me and you."

A silence hung in the air. Both women, rigid and awkward, aware of the fragility of the moment, neither wanting to spark off a full blown argument.

"Well, I hope you'll decide not to," Lecce stated flatly and then got up from the table, adding, "It *will* change things for me. It's bad enough there's a "sir" but I don't think I can do an "old flame" as well."

★★★

Diary Entry

Stayed at the annex all weekend and sulked. I put the answer phone on and did nothing but watch rubbish telly and walk the dog.

At last, by Wednesday night, I decided I was being childish and so left work early on Thursday. I brought Dian a big bunch of flowers and a box of chocolates, promising myself that I would be a reasonable human being. That this was something we could talk about.

The house was empty, but had that "left in a hurry" feel about it. There were dust motes filtering through the lace curtains and the still half-closed long drapes. It was much warmer inside than out. The place was gloomy and stifling so I opened the curtains and one of the sash windows and looked out at the long curve of the road.

I could just see her red Honda jeep about half way down. It was parked under the light-green canopy of a particularly pretty Rowan and I could not help but remember the joyfulness of our romantic, shy, first evening when we had looked out at those trees together, when they were just ghostly and bare-branched silhouettes in the late winter's night.

I couldn't help myself! I walked round the house looking for what – clues? Well it wasn't hard to find them. There were half-drunk glasses of wine in the kitchen sink and fully closed curtains in the bedroom. And two chunky glass candles on the bedside table.

I honestly could not remember those candles and neither of us drinks wine as a rule. So, I waited and waited and fumed and fumed! I think I should have gone home or back to work but I felt somehow paralysed. What is it Shakespeare says about jealousy? Oh yes, the "*green-eyed monster which doth mock: the meat it feeds on*". That was me alright!

She eventually got in about six by which time the flowers had begun to wilt. During the wait, my wild imaginings had been populated with a thousand lurid images. One of which was of me ripping the flowers (or was it old flame?) into pieces and watching the petals (or his dripping blood?) fall onto the bedroom floor! Oh, what melodrama and what fools love makes of us all! (or me anyway.)

I was not that reasonable human being! I demanded to know about the curtains and the candles and the wine glasses, before she had even had a chance to put down her bags.

She looked flustered, and rather less than pleased to see me. Although I had a key I had never gone into her house without being expected before. I suddenly felt in the wrong rather than wronged. I had invaded her private space in a way that she would hate. She had told me that this was her little nook, her nest, the true home of her heart: the only place where she could be completely alone and allow herself to be happy or sad, and drop her "court jester act" and I had trampled all over it.

Without a word, Dian proceeded to make us a pot of tea, choosing the animal teapot and cups we had picked up in a crazy little corner gift shop in Bath and answered my wild questioning evenly, although there was a high colour to her usually creamy, almost flawless complexion.

She said the curtains hadn't been opened this morning and the candles had been there for weeks. She also said that Wendy and Jim from next door had called in yesterday afternoon, to thank her for feeding their cats, bringing the wine. She hadn't got round to washing and putting the glasses away yet. (later, when I peeked into the sink I could see three glasses!)

We sat at the table for a long, long time, neither of us knowing what to say next, watching the sun begin to fade and slide, dusky-orange, behind the backdrop of the tall narrow houses opposite. As the light green of the trees slowly turned grey under the phosphorus street lights, we sat on listening to the raucous cries of roosting birds and above their din the blackbird, on his lamp post perch, begin his sweet goodnight song.

Eventually, I apologised for coming into her house uninvited and she apologised for not seeming pleased to see me. She said, she was pleased, very pleased, and I said I was sorry, very sorry for barging into her house. I promised never, ever, to do it again.

Finally, she said, with a ghost of her wicked smile, "Let's go to bed for a bit, kid."

Yet tonight, now it's Friday, and I am on my own all weekend, staying in the granny flat as Eve, (rather unkindly calls it) with too much time to brood, I can't help thinking about "sir" and "old flame" and hating them both. I can't help thinking that perhaps nothing has been forgotten, or forgiven, by either of us.

Was Grace right when she said that I wouldn't like this kind of love affair for long? I can't help thinking that I gave up so much for someone who seems to give up so little. And I wonder sometimes about Dian. (Yes: Dian, who is she?)

But I still want this love to last, and last and last!

Oh, I hope I do!

CHAPTER EIGHT

The Past

Lecce

Lecce experienced a glow of deep relief and an almost perfect happiness as she unlocked the door of the familiar, crowded room. It was good to get away from her private life and feel in control again. Work made perfect sense and it was a great place to hide.

She threw her briefcase onto the desk and inhaled the musty air of their century old building. It was untidy but homely. Reception, was chock full of every essential piece of office equipment Jenny and Rose believed that they just could not do without.

Whilst Lecce insisted that the strange, although not unpleasant smell was the positive aroma of generational education, people, like Billy, insisted the house was haunted. Well, caretakers will wander around locking up when everyone else has long gone. The odd creaks and sudden squeals of hinges and doors swinging inexplicably shut were no more than just draughts through the missing tiles from the roof: unless it was the old house putting itself to bed – or waking up.

For once she was first in. Usually she would be greeted by Jenny and Rose who travelled to work together and liked to spend the first hour working in companionable silence. Jenny seemed to truly enjoy putting her post to rights and checking the answer phone. Rose, who was in charge of petty cash, was meticulous in sharing out the change into the red, dented cash tin.

Looking over at her unsorted post, she wondered if she dare pick up a letter or two before Jenny arrived. Glancing through the window, she saw the two women hurriedly crossing the grass area from the car park. She dropped the pile back onto her in tray, grinning and waving guiltily, repressing a childlike desire to hide her hands behind her back!

Both had the same purposeful stride but otherwise they could not look more dissimilar. Rose was at least six, if not eight inches taller; statuesque and ebony-skinned, her hair in tight African bangs. Today she wore an eye-catching bright orange jacket and a long brown skirt with a pair of death-defying heels. Lecce sighed, how nice to be tall and have a wardrobe full of such peacock-colours.

She could see that Jenny had altered her hair shade again. Dare she comment on the ear length *auburn* bob? No – better not! There would be a sniff and a denial that anything was changed. Well, the sensible flat crocs and the navy trousers and waistcoat were certainly the same.

Lecce loved these two women. Although nominally the boss, she thought of their trio as more of a friendly team who problem solved together on the hoof, from the moment the clock struck nine until they stumbled homeward, often well after seven.

As the two bustled through the door, Rose lifted her expressive eyebrows in surprise, "new boss! How come you're in before us?"

Lecce was always quick to laugh off Rose's nickname, yet inside still felt a small glow of shy pleasure and surprise. This was her dream job and one she had never thought to win.

★★★

Letter from Karin Pedersen

Dear Lecce,

I am just enquiring about my next contract. Will I be offered the same hours, including the assessments? They are from 4pm – to 6pm.

How are you? I hear you had to have a small operation on your hand. I hope you are feeling better.

Best Regards
Karin Pedersen

Lecce

Lecce read the letter with a mixture of amusement and perplexity. It must have been placed in her in tray before half term and was written on a sheet of exercise paper and in green ink! She struggled hard to picture this Karin. Erica had taken on a few extra staff when she was on sick leave. Would Erica have overlooked issuing a contract? If she had forgotten, surely Rose or Jenny would have picked it up and sent down a reminder?

The letter was innocuous, but still, there was something disconcerting about its look and seemingly innocent questions. Perhaps it was just the weird use of green ink, or did she feel guilty because she just could not place this member of her staff?

With an intrigued sense of purpose, she crossed to the tall filing cabinet and wrenched open the stiff drawer helpfully labelled personnel records. The contract and CV were neatly stapled to the inside of the file. She stared hard at the small passport-sized photograph of a blond, blue-eyed young woman with a fetching shy smile: still no bells rang.

She studied the details, noting the nationality and was impressed. It would take a special kind of resilience to move across the globe, get educated and employed at such a young age. Was twenty-six really that young? From her two decades of distance it certainly seemed that way. Would she have been able to do what this Karin Pedersen had done?

She had not even known what a CV was then! She was already married with a young child and another on the way. Lecce felt a small twinge of envy. Her own life had taken so many awkward twists and turns before education and curriculum vitae had meant anything to her.

Her mind wandered to her children and she allowed herself a fleeting moment of pleasure and pride. At least they, like this Karin Pedersen, had been given opportunities denied to most of her own working-class generation. It had been a struggle, but somehow she and Grace had managed to support them right through to university and they definitely knew what a CV was.

Returning to Karin's credentials, she had to admit that they were impressive; perhaps rather too impressive for a part time teaching position. Her areas of expertise were not languages either. They were subjects you might expect from someone dreaming of a life in the diplomatic service or as a political journalist. Lecce pictured those rather drab clad women on the serious news programmes. Karin's fragile looks certainly did not fit that picture, although she might look good in a flak jacket! What could have caused such a sea change in ambition? Now she was just being … what was she being?

That was definitely not her business but her patchy work experience might be. No more than four months in any one place, and most were for just a month or two. Maybe she was finishing her studies? Had Erica not followed up on the references either? She scribbled a note to Rose asking her to check, all the while questioning why she should feel an element of creeping unease.

Lecce sat for a while, staring down at the quirky green-penned letter and the extraordinarily thin working history. Maybe all that short-term work was the reason for the young woman's anxiety about a contract for next year. If she was keen to settle in one place now, perhaps all she needed was some reassurance? Lecce picked up the phone but then replaced it. For some unfathomable reason, she was loath to call and just as reluctant to write. Eventually she decided to stop playing detective and wait until the first day of the new term and introduce herself properly to Karin and the other new members with a formal staff meeting.

★★★

Diary Entry

The three of us were so proud of the way we had organised the staff meeting, we fist bumped on the way in! We had everyone sitting down ***on time*** and, for once, all the handouts were organised and ready. I had only uttered the fateful words, "Thanks for coming everyone. Let's get started, shall we" before there was an almighty crashing to the left and as I looked up I saw that Karin Pedersen had pushed her chair back so hard that it had ricocheted off the wall and clattered to the floor! Then she practically ran from the room leaving the rest of us staring after her. Her partner, Jack, just got busy opening his notebook and putting on his glasses.

For a mini second or two there was this awful silence and I felt all eyes (apart from that Jack's) swivel in my direction. So, I said ***very brightly***, "Let's turn to item one on the agenda."

Later, over the tea and cakes, I asked Jack if Karin was ok and he said with, what I thought was a forced casualness, "Oh yes, I know what that's all about," and picked up a piece of Swiss roll and made as if to turn away.

So I tried again, "Don't you think you should go and see if she's alright? Rose said she thinks she was heading for the car park."

He poured himself another cup of tea and mumbled unenthusiastically, "In a bit … maybe."

I think they must have had some kind of argument; his face looked rather strained and tired. I noticed then that he must be quite a lot older than her (my age?). I'm being mean now, but he did look a bit like my Dad with his receding hairline and that awful baggy cardigan! Although to be fair to my Dad, ***his*** cardigan doesn't have holes, as Mum would never allow it!

Anyway, Rose made me go out to the car park and there she was, lying in the back seat covered in a blanket! I would have knocked on the window but she had somehow contrived to make herself into the most unapproachable shape imaginable, even her head was covered. In this heat!

When I told Rose, she just said, in that disapproving way she has sometimes,

"Well, we can't pay her. She didn't sign the register."

I expect she thinks I should have rapped on the window and had "words" with the girl for rushing out like that. I didn't authorise the attendance payment. I didn't have the nerve! Should I have done more? Surely it was up to Jack – the poor thing!

Well, I certainly know who Karin Pedersen is now!

Was it something I said?

CHAPTER NINE

Lecce & Karin

Every evening around four o'clock, Lecce would find time to sneak outside and sit for a while in the old and faded Victorian garden space. At that time of day, the benches were empty and the outdoors was strangely silent of people-noise for a while. On a good day it was such a pleasing respite from all the dimly lit corridors and their particularly stuffy and cramped basement office.

With a feeling of luxurious ease, she spread out the centrefold of her newspaper and sipped her tea, half listening to the constant chorus of small birds that had lived forever within the ivy clad hollows of the red brick walls.

Throughout this unusually sun-filled month she had ardently wished she had not agreed to move downstairs with Erica. It was true, as had been quite firmly pointed out, there were far less distractions and more of the tedious paperwork did get done. She was slowly, if grudgingly, coming to appreciate having Erica and all her experience at hand to help solve a never-ending stream of thorny predicaments. But she sorely missed Jenny and Rose and the entire hectic jaw dropping activity that was reception.

Still, now she had more time, this daily golden opportunity to sit alone in the open air and sun herself for a few moments was almost worth the daily exaggerated sense of imprisonment in their basement office.

In the shadow of an upstairs window, half hidden by a broken blind, a slender figure, Karin Pedersen, was curiously contemplating the woman, her boss, she supposed, sitting on the bench.

She liked the way Lecce's short fringe of shiny blond tinted hair fell across her eyes as she bent to read the newspaper. She admired the confident posture and the sexy sunglasses.

Lecce always seemed to achieve a careless kind of smartness. Today she was in a white open-necked shirt, and slim fitting grey slacks that complimented shiny black ankle boots. She was no expert, but it was almost certain that Lecce was gay. As she continued to stare down into the garden at the older woman, she casually wondered what was making her hide behind the blind and get quite hot about someone of the same sex.

Karin had discovered that this unique small department of part-time teachers were a loyal bunch, not much given to gossip, and she had not had that assumption confirmed. Lecce was popular with the staff and a frequent visitor to the lunch room where she often joined in with the wise cracks or occasionally, the more serious discussions. Karin had found herself covertly watching her, a little fascinated, wanting an opportunity to join in and attract her attention, but a surprising shyness always left her tongue-tied.

For a few minutes she kept one eye on the woman at the garden bench and the other on packing her old brown satchel. As she saw Lecce folding the paper and making a move, Karin only hesitated for a fraction before decisively making a move.

"Hello, Lecce!" Karin was a little breathless, having taken the three flights down at breakneck speed. "Do you think the school traffic has died down a bit now?" That was lame. It would have to do.

Lecce glanced up, taking a second to place the younger woman, noting the natural almost white blond ear length hair and the fetching smile she had observed in the photograph. She also recalled that clattering chair and the panicky rush from the room. It was that enigma, Karin Pedersen.

"If you leave now, you'll probably miss the workplace rush hour!" She gave a lopsided grin and a raise of an eyebrow, in what she hoped was an approachable manner. She thought that perhaps she should mention the unresponsive referees but instead added,

"In this heat you'll probably have to keep both windows all the way down!"

Karin nodded and shrugged with a small self-deprecating sigh, "I'm used to it. I've only got an old banger. I bet you've got really good air conditioning."

Lecce laughed, trying to picture her Dad's old cast-off Ford, with anything remotely like a working fan and said, "No, but the roof opens!"

There were still some leaving sounds of slamming of doors and the turnover of engines from the gradually emptying car park. Karin, wanting to prolong their conversation, said quickly, "Can I see your car?"

"You want to see my car?" Lecce repeated and picked up her paper, vaguely flattered and intrigued. "Ok, why not?"

They crossed the grassy area Karin swinging her bag in that rather endearing way Lecce remembered her children had done when meeting her at the school gates. As they reached the pathway and Lecce searched for her car, she stopped mid-stride and gave a small embarrassed laugh.

She had clean forgotten all about the pigeons that regularly colonised the tree she had parked under this morning. The dark blue, the door handles and all the windows were covered in white splatters.

"Oh shit!" Lecce flushed, "Oops, sorry for the s word!"

"What else could you say?" Karin's laugh was deep and throaty and for the first time their eyes met. Lecce realised with a start that this young woman was a lot more than just the tempestuous girl she had thought her to be. Those light blue eyes sparked and held onto her own for just a little too long, seeming to ask a question and to offer the kind of challenge she had only ever met from women in her own world.

Surprised by a faint blush, she hurriedly stepped away and began a desperate hunt through her pockets for a handkerchief.

"Perhaps these will be of help?" Karin calmly held out a small bottle of water and some tissues.

★★★

As Lecce rocked under the huge soap-filled mechanical brushes of the car wash, she reflected on their unexpected ten minutes of shared hilarious laughter. They had worked together, clearing the windscreen, alternately muttering, "Shit! Shit! Shit!"

Not so long ago she and Dian would have found it equally as ludicrous, but they were not laughing much these days. Her high spirits abruptly dropped and like a broken needle on an old 45 she became stuck on the ever-present simmering grudges against "sir" and "old flame." Her mood nose-dived to zero. In a sudden burst of frustration she reached out to the radio and switched on the news, deciding she was sick of their old love songs and was not going to call in on Dian after all.

Karin had meant to drive straight home but instead had parked across the road behind a battered set of petrol pumps in an old disused petrol station. She had to get that edgy exhilarated feeling under control. There was also an overpowering need to catch another glimpse of Lecce. She wanted to think about what that might mean. She had thought all of that was gone for good. Last time had turned into such a mess. She had decided it was safer to settle for steady old Jack, but now? Well, now she was not so sure.

Looking into those dark blue eyes had been fascinating, a real turn on. Lecce was a woman, but what was so wrong with that? As she considered what lesbian sex might be and what it might be like to kiss Lecce Connor, she felt a little shiver of excitement and wondered if it was possible she could be in love, whatever love was of course.

It was over an hour before Karin saw Lecce and her bird splattered car turn at the exit. She stared after the retreating pigeon-painted break lights and felt another frisson of excitement and anticipation. There was a definite connection between them. Lecce must have felt it too.

The water and tissues had been one of those serendipity moments: perhaps they were meant to be? At the very least, those arresting eyes would no longer drift unseeingly over her and pass onto someone else more interesting.

It was risky. Jack was always on the watch since Greg, but he would never imagine she would go for a woman. Oh yes, she did want to go for it. She wanted Lecce and well, she could have her if she tried. She could always have anyone, if she tried hard enough. This time, maybe it would work out. Lecce was going to be different. She twisted the radio dial and found Radio One. As she pulled away, she speculated about Lecce and what music she listened to, deciding it must be something better than Jack's old seventies favourites. Those two might be the same age, but Lecce was so far removed from Jack that they might as well be on different planets!

Diary Entry

Karin was in the car park tonight. She just seemed to appear from nowhere! It was past six. "Late leaving?" I asked. She smiled that unexpected lovely smile and said, "Just stalking you!" I grinned weakly. It did feel a bit like that!

Then she asked if she could sit in my car for a few minutes with me. She was thinking of getting a tape player in hers and wanted to know how mine worked. I played Mr Jones by Counting Crows. Dian described it once as the "howls of a demented druggie!" But Karin actually liked it and asked if I could do a copy for her, so I gave her that one.

I expect Erica would call that "fraternising with the staff!"

Diary Entry

Karin stayed late yet again! She brought me out a cup of tea and as we were drinking it and I was trying to think of something to say, she suddenly asked, "What's in your briefcase?"

"That's a strange question," I said. "Why would you want to know that?"

She said, "You can learn a lot about a person if you see what's in their bag."

That's never occurred to me. Am I just too reserved and British? I said, "Show me what's in *your* bag and then I might."

"You show me yours and I'll show you mine."

Was she flirting with me – oh dear, I hope not!!

I emptied my case. There was just the usual; my battered diary, a carton of milk, the *Daily Mirror*, a few pens and my two mobile phones.

"Do you always drink milk and read the *Daily Mirror*?" she said in that seductive hoarse flirty tone she has.

"Yes. Don't you?" (I hope I wasn't being flirty back, but it ***is*** hard to resist.)

She said, "That's really quite sweet," and emptied her bag. It only had a few practice exam papers to mark, two registers, a ragged, zip-up pencil case and a nondescript grey purse.

Nothing to learn about her from that then!

Diary Entry

Somehow I found myself telling Karin about Dian and "sir" and the "old flame". When she suggested that I could always change "sir" to "cur" and "old flame" to "old fucker" I found myself sniggering like a teenager!

Oh, I know it's unprofessional, but I am so fed up with keeping it all to myself, and furious that Dian just absolutely refuses to touch either subject. We just start a kind of polite bickering. I never win. It's almost an art form with her. No wonder I keep making excuses to work late and then go home to Mum and Dad, so cosily a twosome.

Now I'm spending more time in it, the annex is really quite ok, especially as the French doors mean I can walk straight out to the pond Dad and I made last year. The bedroom still has shelves full of Granddad's clothes and Grandma's awful giant rose-petal curtains. Not to mention the matching sofa in the sitting room! It's got their bed too, now my bed. Mum was born in that bed. Imagine that! No don't! In my present mood, I'm finding those things of theirs really rather comforting. I still miss them, and I do miss Dian, but I don't think we like each other very much these days.

I wish Eve wouldn't make so many jokes about me living in a granny flat. It makes me feel like a bit of a failure. I don't always like Eve.

I don't feel very likeable. I feel jealous, and suspicious and unsure where I fit into Dian's life. (Oh yes, and I sometimes feel quite murderous like that awful Lady Macbeth!)

Karin seems to like me, at least. She's very conscientious and spends ages preparing lessons before she goes home. Since the "bird shit incident" (as we call it) she often brings me out a cup of tea in a mug she gave me. It's covered in ridiculous green, bug-eyed frogs! We sit out at the bench on our square of patchy grass, just chatting and joking about, sometimes for an hour or more. I asked her once about needing to get home to Jack and she looked away, her face suddenly unreadable and strained. She just mumbled something about there being no rush, and she was enjoying herself in the garden with me. That it was good to have someone to have fun with for a change.

I told her on Friday I was finding all the different exam dates complicated and today she brought me in an exam planner format she'd found at a book shop over the weekend. How nice is that? How thoughtful, and she offered to help me, but I won't ask.

Karin suggested I should ring her over the weekend if I'm lonely. But I can't. Somehow, I don't think Erica would approve. She thinks we should be approachable but "a little distant". But I have to say Karin is very good for my battered ego, and if she likes me a bit too much then it's only a little crush.

Oh, I hope it is!

CHAPTER TEN

Lecce

Present Day

As Lecce ate her porridge she considered the untidy heap of paper stacked on her workbench. These were her only written record of those "Dian Days". She looked at the scruffy old blue diary, with the peeling photographs on the front cover and smiled. All those early love-smitten writings scrawled and full of excitement, so full of question and exclamation marks!

There were the postcards, some from their brief holiday in Bath and a few yellowing envelopes containing letters Dian had written from abroad. Beneath all of those were a handful of poem fragments along with half a dozen pages of a hilarious attempt at a steamy lesbian liaison they had written in the style of Jane Austin!

All only half remembered … at first there had been a lot of laughter, a lot of playful and loving sex, and then there had been those snakes in their Eden: "sir" and "old flame": her jealousy and Dian's determined evasiveness.

Everything had gradually fizzled out between them after that telephone call from the mysterious "sir."Eventually she had accepted that Dian had meant what she had always said: "I'm married and I will always be married. It's what I want."

She struggled to revisit her feelings back then. She had a hazy recollection of disappointment, regret, resignation, a few tears and lonely evenings.

No, it was not Dian she had wanted to forget. It was not their love affair she had deliberately packed away, out of sight, if not quite out of mind. Their early romance had, with very little effort become a close friendship that had never wavered. Even she and Grace, with a lot more work on both sides, had re-forged a new strong and loving bond which was still important to the both of them.

Why would those miss-steps and disappointments come back to haunt her now? There were far more envelopes and other paper mementoes than those from Grace and Dian in the box. It was the others she had delayed reading, those she always pushed aside into a corner or under the diary whenever they revealed themselves: bulky brown envelopes, postcards by the dozens, and an uncountable number of coloured envelopes and her name, sometimes in capitals, occasionally just her initials, but always, always written in a strange hand and with a green pen.

Lecce gave an involuntary start and leaned back on her chair, as if she could push away a name that flitted and then evaporated like an unwelcome spectre. She flinched as a sudden rush of a long-buried memory gave her another glimpse of a pale face and white blond hair, of changeable light blue eyes that in an instant seemed to spark with either heat or ice.

Lecce felt her heart start to race with that nervous fluttering. With frantic determination, she pushed back that name. Shutting down that face, that love, that kind of love that dare not speak its name, until every harrowing encroaching thought finally ebbed away and the panic faded.

As she sat on, far into the morning, ignoring the cat's cries and the everyday tasks that needed her urgent attention, she forced out a series of questions: how and why had she so successfully suppressed her own autobiography by merely storing away old letters and a diary? Who was that other someone? What had she done by taking down that box and dragging everything out into the light of her quiet, ordered world? Did she have the courage to open herself to whatever hurts sat waiting for her?

CHAPTER ELEVEN

A blond, too young woman, smiling.
Standing at the foot of the stairs in
a dashing red shirt.
"Oh, your hair is cut!" I said
she blushed shirt-red – and I
If truth be told.

Later in our office, Rose said with an amused (or not so amused?) smile. "That young woman wants to do something bad with you!"

I was glad my face was in the filing cabinet!
Seriously! Oh crap! Plank!

Diary Entry

Karin is away and there has only been one message left by Jack that said she was "under the weather". Hope it's not serious. Lots of summer colds now the weather's changed. Erica was a little snippy and pointed out that staff must notify us on a "daily basis". She wasn't happy about the term "under the weather" either.

Is that what's wrong with me? Am I just under the weather?

Diary Entry

I was covering the phone this afternoon so Jenny and Rose could have a break and picked up a call from Karin. I was pleased to hear from her, I think I've missed her (?) but she sounded very subdued.

She said she didn't want to discuss anything on the phone but could I have lunch with her on Friday if she came in, so she could explain. I said all she needed to do was bring in a self certificate but she said, sounding a bit desperate, "Please have lunch with me, Lecce. I really need to talk to you." So I agreed and told her to bring an umbrella as the nearest cafe is at least ten minutes away. This rain looks like it is never going to stop. All that lovely weather seems a long way off. **Pants!**

★★★

Lecce and Karin

They splashed towards the cafe in an almost silence, only sharing a few desultory words about the weather. It was far too noisy to say much and they were kept busy dodging the muddy puddle spray from speeding traffic. A mother, with a pushchair and a grizzling infant hanging onto her coat, rushed around them with a muttered curse and a desperate look of panic. Karin felt a flash of irritation; the British were so obsessed with rain! She was quite happy to pull up her hood, put her hands in her pockets, and get on with it.

She was consumed with an unusual impatience and wondered if they would ever reach the wretched place. Maybe she should have suggested sandwiches and an empty room instead. A wave of unease swept over her. She was rushing things but if she waited too long and didn't initiate something, maybe Lecce would get back with that Dian.

Instinctively, though, she realised that these few intimate moments under Jack's umbrella could be significant. They were, by necessity, huddled quite cosily together and that was good, in fact, it felt very good. They had linked arms and Karin was enjoying the difference in their height, finding reasons to lean down and allow her fringe to occasionally brush the shorter woman's cheek.

Lecce felt a small twinge of consternation as they entered. These old greasy spoons, once so familiar on most city street corners, were now becoming a rarity and on days like today she understood why.

The air was steamy and smelt of raincoat, damp dog and chip fat. Squeezing into the only available space opposite the kitchen door, she noticed the plastic table cloth was sticky and the sauce bottles grubby. In the background was an indecipherable tinny radio. Could it get any worse?

She raised her eyebrows, grinning and began to frame an apology but stopped short as she registered the translucent blue paleness beneath Karin's eyes, her hollowed cheekbones, and a barely healed scab on her lower lip. If possible, her slight frame seemed to have morphed into near emaciation within only a few days.

"What on earth is wrong?" she said. "I hate to say it but you look awful!" she added impulsively reaching across and taking hold of the thin fingers, which she could now see were bitten quite to the quick.

"We need to talk," Karin replied, her voice urgent and halting. She took her hands away and reached into an inside pocket, pulling out a long bulky brown envelope. Lecce saw her name printed in light green, and recalled vaguely the note she had received a while back about work and contracts.

"Oh, is that a resignation letter?" Lecce reacted cautiously, caught out by a sudden dart of disappointment.

"Jack wants to move to Preston, if he gets this job. I don't! I said he could go on his own. He won't get it anyway, he never gets the job."

Lecce looked up, surprised and disconcerted by the tone of sudden vehemence. Was this why she had been off sick, why she looked so ill? Perhaps she and Jack were breaking up? Her mind frantically began to hunt for the appropriate words, reflecting that Dian or Erica would know just what to say.

"It's a letter for you." Karin carefully propped the letter against the sauce bottles. "I thought I would write as I'm no good at saying things. It's about us."

"Us?" Lecce could only echo. There was a small silence as she attempted to process the significance of that word. At the same time, she became acutely conscious of her companion's knees pressing against her own. The pressure was light but still, it felt insistent, deliberate. Embarrassed, Lecce tried to shuffle her chair back but the wall behind gave her little room. Karin's legs were much longer than hers. The space available was limited, so surely this must be accidental? A warm flush swept down from her neck and with a shock, she realised that her treacherous body was responding with an inexplicable rush of heat between her legs.

Lecce stood up hastily and said, "I had better get us a cup of tea and order something to eat, or they'll be chucking us out."

Karin shrugged and nodded, asked for tea and toast and watched Lecce with a covert ghost of a smile, as she hurried to join the messy queue that was now spilling over into the open doorway.

Karin had seen Lecce colour; had picked up on the chemistry. With a thrill she realised that with just a little more persuasion, she could have her. For once, though, it was not just the excitement and the challenge, or even curiosity to find out what it was like to have a woman.

As she watched Lecce patiently waiting in the queue, she realised that she also craved this other woman's warmth, her kindness. Perhaps this time, this someone, could fill what she knew to be her own stubbornly empty heart. Once she had thought Jack was the one to do that, but now she was not so sure. It felt good, really good to have this overwhelming surge again, even if with, or maybe because, it was with a woman.

Lecce spent a few minutes busily distributing their lunch from the tray, suddenly aware that she had lost any appetite for the toasted cheese and tomato sandwich before her. Bewildered and scandalized by her inexplicable sexual arousal in a crowded public place, she peeked furtively at her fellow diners seated only a few feet away. Thankfully, they were all innocently reading the paper or hurriedly gulping down their congealing egg and chips.

Taking refuge behind her chipped mug of stewed tea, she realised she would have to respond somehow. There must be something sensible, something diplomatic to say that would not sound incredulous or dishonest. I like you very much as a friend but … I'm flattered but … How nice of you but … how could she deny the obvious magnetic sexual tension that was once again passing back and forth between them?

Finally, she ventured, "Karin, I can't pretend there isn't an attraction, but us?"

Karin leaned across the table, and asked with a slight tremble to her lower lip, "You do like me, don't you? I'm sure you do, and it feels like us to me." Lecce did not try and move when that slight pressure from those slim jean-clad legs once more insinuated themselves between her own and for a long moment, her eyes held onto the intensity of Karin's stare.

Abruptly Karin broke the spell by slowly moving each leg away, luxuriously stretching them into the now empty aisle. Lecce was shocked to find she had been completely unaware of the steady exodus that had been going on around them. The majority of the cafe's former occupants had disappeared and even the confused static of the radio had ceased. She had been in some kind of oblivious haze, wallowing in a pool of an unwelcome, yet intoxicating desire.

She turned away in confusion, noting the long steely hands of the grease-spattered clock face clacking noisily towards two. Turning back, she was grateful to find there was just a pretty young woman with an unnaturally pale and wan face seated before her. That luminous, other-world apparition of only moments earlier had thankfully disappeared.

"We'll have to leave soon, Karin," she said, suddenly firmly in control. "It's not only Jack, is it? There are a thousand other impossibilities. I could write you a dozen bullet point lists if you like! For example, you do realise that, unfortunately, I am old enough to be your mother?" and she laughed, trying to lighten the still charged atmosphere that hovered, aware that the woman behind the counter was giving them a curious look as she piled dirty plates and rattled knives and forks into the dishwasher.

"Age!" Karin gave a dismissive shrug. "That's just a number on a birth certificate. My last boyfriend was fifty-three, so that makes you still young!"

Lecce pushed aside her half-eaten lunch and slowly, but decisively, shook her head. In her heart she knew that she had never really approved of wide age gaps, had found it hard not to voice that objection when Sal had casually introduced her to a much older man. It had been Grace that had counselled caution, saying it would fizzle out, which of course it had.

"I'm really sorry, Karin. I hope we can stay friends," she said, feeling suddenly stuffy and middle aged," I really do like you, oh dear, in fact, I think I must like you a bit too much, but we both have to accept that this would be madness."

"At least read my letter," Karin replied and handed Lecce the envelope, giving her fingers a quick squeeze. "Think about it. We only live once. You told me that. I know it looks long, but I've enclosed a short story I like. I just wanted to share it with you."

Karin began to pick at a finger, realising with a start that she was genuinely anxious in case she had let her advantage slip away. "Please, Lecce. It's only a letter and a short story. It won't bite!"

Lecce studied the childlike earnest expression and the pallid, ethereal slightness of the young woman opposite and immediately felt embarrassed, guilty and strangely culpable. As she put the envelope in her bag, she was already thinking that to take it was a mistake but to actually read it could turn into a real can of worms.

And even then, on their desultory walk back to work, she gabbling and Karin morose and crestfallen, she had already known that she would read it. Her fingers literally itched until Erica left for her meeting.

As soon as the door closed Lecce reached for her bag and took out the letter, uncomfortable in the knowledge that Erica's censure would be damning and heavy and justified.

"Don't be such a fool Lecce Connor!" she muttered, but opened it all the same.

CHAPTER TWELVE

Present Day

Lecce

Lecce had left her car at the allotment and was now on foot, making her way to the Community Library, still fretful with indecision acutely aware that with every downhill step, she was creating a satisfying distance between herself and the box. The waste bin had been primed with kindling and firelighters, old newspapers and magazines. It was a dry, wind-free day and all that was needed was just a decisive strike from one of the extra-large Swan matches.

She had, just for the moment anyway, abandoned the burning and was hurriedly walking through the old village back lanes. With an effort, she forced her gloomy preoccupations to drift and to focus instead on the crumbling stone-walled gardens, the wildflowers in the hedgerows, the indistinct and pleasing sounds of kitchen radios and playing children.

Once inside, she admired afresh the stark contrast between this recently refurbished structure and its comfortable welcoming atmosphere to the original. That had been draft-ridden, all polished wood, buffed linoleum and a strictly enforced silence policy, only occasionally broken by a whispered question or the muted click of a date stamp.

Her intention was to create a diversion for a little thinking time. To try and dampen the surprisingly sickening dread which the sight of her name printed in an uneven green-penned script had caused. She would swap her audio books, pick up some more recycle bags and perhaps exchange an innocuous word or two with the friendly librarians.

Her earlier agitation began to calm as for the first time she observed the uncanny likeness between Lindsey and Maxine to her former colleagues, Jenny and Rose. They had the same distinctly differing heights and dress sense, but worked together in a harmony only possible with people who had found a way to happily co-exist inside a small space.

There were plenty of people using the library, most of them seated in front of the newly installed computers. Waiting in line, she began to glance idly about her and soon grew envious of the occupants who were seated in front of their respective screens confidently scrolling down or rapidly tapping keyboards.

As she reached the desk, Maxine smiled a greeting and quickly completed a request slip using the green nib from a bulky multi-coloured novelty pen. An unexpected shy resolve prompted Lecce to lay aside her books and ask instead whether there was time to explain how to use this research thing called Google.

For a while Lecce was diverted, intrigued by how easy it was to find her way around what Maxine had told her was a search engine. She busily looked up word meanings and spellings until she eventually tired of avoiding her real purpose for wanting to know about Google.

Staring at the inviting box on her screen, her mind slowly began to frame a series of questions. Why did her memory provide the colour and the shape of the words so clearly yet leave the content so blank, so void? Why would the sight of them, a mere glimpse of green, create such a reaction? What was so wrong with green ink writing?

Perhaps it would not hurt to ask Mr Google? In an instant, the title "The Green Ink Brigade" in over-large type filled the screen.

Lecce slumped back on her seat with a barely restrained gasp, trying in vain to compose herself. She scanned and rescanned the article. Could there really be such people as the lone green ink writer? Someone whose obsession drove them to write compulsively to the chosen object of her or his attention?

Those letters, so many and so green! At first, she had thought them quirky and flattering and, she was certain, they puzzled and excited her with their flowery compliments and suggestive sexual undertones.

But today, the very sight of all those letters with her name often written in heavily printed capitals, had caused her to cry out and pull her hand away as if bitten by a snake! There had been a hurtling memory rush of kaleidoscopic images of green ink scrawl; her name on envelopes endlessly dropping through letter boxes or appearing on in trays and desks.

Although a fierce headache had started she continued to scrutinise the article. She noted the date; yes, the same year she had begun an unlikely friendship. Karin! Her stomach churned at the name: Karin Pedersen. She had been the writer of all those letters and was, she now remembered, a very well-qualified journalist. Was it implausible that she would not have known the meaning of green ink?

Finally, Lecce asked for Maxine's help and printed off the text, placing it carefully in her rucksack, deciding that she was going to have to read at least the first remaining letter in the box. They were all no more than papery blanks at the moment but reading them would force her to open up and confront a past that she must have deliberately forgotten for a reason.

As she struggled uphill and back to the allotment Lecce felt a pressing need to be safely indoors where she could sit down and find a calm space inside her wild mind. Once there, she headed straight for her car – there would be nothing more burned today!

★★★

Lecce parked the car at a crazy angle; half in, half out of the garage. She hardly broke her breakneck stride until she reached the conservatory and had dumped the box back onto the table. Not daring to hesitate she pulled out an envelope, quickly putting aside the enclosed photocopied story and hastily read the letter. It was impossible not to question the green-inked, almost illegible hand. Was this the mark of an obsessive, a joker or just a coincidence?

Lecce sat down, ignoring George rubbing his head against her ankles and starting up his motoring purr, hoping for dinner. She soberly reread each word: once, twice, a third time, before throwing it to the floor with a yell of exasperation. All those effusive superlatives! How could she have been so taken in by such patent flattery?

She stood staring down at the green untidy writing with dislike. They had barely known each other. She had a vague memory of flirty chats on a garden bench, perhaps a couple of half confidences. How could any of that have been construed by either of them as an "us"?

But then, there had been that lunch. Surprising tears welled behind her lids as a long-suppressed afternoon swept back into her consciousness. With a shameful clarity that still had the power to sting, she remembered the steamy damp room, the cramped table in a corner and the heat of an expert caress on her thigh which had left her unable to control a disconcerting wave of sexual arousal.

Who had this Karin been? Just the love-struck girl-woman of the letter:

"You are the most wonderful, fascinating, amazing, charming, sexy woman I have ever met!"

Or a knowing enchantress who calmly played sex games beneath a table in a crowded cafe. Who could flatter and smile and play the villain?

Dimly aware that a sharp claw in the present was gently grazing her bare ankle and that the winter daylight had begun to fade, Lecce stopped to pick up George and inhaled his familiar catty smell before resolutely turning her thoughts to the early evening and the many mindless tasks that were awaiting her attention.

Yet within an hour she had deserted her barely touched meal and the whistling kettle and was back in the conservatory. She picked up the fallen diary, her mouth tightening at the effort, and placed it on the workbench. For a long moment she looked at its cover before letting her fingers flick rapidly through the pages until they reached August.

The Past

Diary Entry

What have I done? That cafe! That letter!

So this is what Erica meant when she warned about "fraternising"!

I can hear Dian saying, "You must be crazed!"

And, I ***was*** crazed, at least for a moment in the cafe!

Yes Erica – that ***was*** "over familiar!"

I responded – I know I did!

But I'm not crazed now, and whatever that was – that just isn't me! Is it?

I certainly can't reply to that letter and I definitely won't be having any more lunches!

Thank heavens there's only one week left of the Summer School.

I'm going swimming **and I am going to forget about it!**

CHAPTER THIRTEEN

Lecce

Present Day

Lecce put down the diary with a frown. There was nothing else, just nothing but blank pages for the rest of August and then September through to December. But what was there was damning enough, wasn't it? She had not even had the courage to speak truth to her private self. She had questioned Karin's motives but now there were questions she needed to ask of herself. Had she done something so shameful she dare not remember? Had she, the elder in a position of trust, taken advantage of an impressionable and vulnerable much younger woman?

She began to leaf through each date, unable to accept that she had so wilfully and resolutely not recorded her actions after that afternoon. Finally, just a few pages from the end she found a single entry in a hand so cramped and small and so unlike her own.

She stood stock still, gripping the final pages of the diary, fighting the return of that weakness, that fluttery fear bird feeling in the pit of her stomach. No! She could not read that now but, sooner or later she would, she knew she would.

That decision, delayed since the box came down was made. The choice to remember or not had been taken away when she had withheld that match this morning, when she had searched "green writing" this afternoon, when she had read that letter and picked up the diary this evening!

And so she sat, long into the evening, searching her obdurate mind for every pitiless detail, for a long time oblivious to the fading warmth inside the conservatory. Eventually, with a slight shiver, she closed the French doors and drifted to the windowsill where she lit the half dozen tea lights. She sat on and on vaguely watching them from her seat in the shadowed corner as they flickered and reflected back from the wide picture windows.

Wanting to divert her thoughts with pleasant memories, she thought back to the younger Keith. They had always loved to watch the spectacle of the bats together. He had often called them "The Luftwaffe!" From May on, through the whole summer and early autumn they had sat mesmerized by the sight of so many dark quick-winged bodies invading their night-time garden skies; marvelling at their frantic aerial sorties, swooping and darting, miraculously avoiding each other and the glass: ruthlessly hunting for their hapless insect prey.

An unwanted connection between the bats and the discarded short story from the envelope came creeping into her mind. She had recognised it as one from a book of unsettling tales about life as a wartime fighter pilot during World War ll. She remembered quickly refolding the pages and returning it to the envelope, deciding not to dwell on the content or the possible reason behind Karin choosing to share such an appalling story.

She had never really enjoyed the writings of Roald Dahl, not even his amusing but somehow ghastly twisted stories for children. Keith and Sal had dragged her with them to watch the awful Matilda. She had sat silent and horrified, as seemingly, every child in the darkened cinema, chortled with glee, not turning a hair at the tyrannical punishments of the psychopathic Head Teacher, Trunchbull. He had been a genius-but still …

What had been the gist of that story, The Airman? There had been an undercurrent of something far darker and far more sinister than a frantic air battle. It was much more than just a vivid description of two men fighting for their own survival: a midair collision and a falling safely to earth had somehow culminated instead into a cowardly, senseless murder. A murder made ridiculous by a panic-ridden struggle in a muddy cow pond, leaving the reader shocked and unsure of the identity of the survivor.

Why had Karin taken the trouble to photocopy every page and then include it in what was meant to be a love letter? Had she chosen it as a ...premonition, a prophecy, a warning? An inevitable ending to whatever there had been between them? Had she already planned the end at the beginning?

With a shudder Lecce sat upright, the diary dropped onto the floor, half covering the discarded letter. There was a tugging at her mind and heart: a wanting to recoil away from the past: to create a definite distance from the box and from her now insistent memories. Yet, she knew that another part of her needed, to reclaim that truth. And not just about Karin but also about herself. ***It was time to remember!***

End of Part One

Part Two

"You've been hit by - you've been struck by a smooth criminal"
Bad, Michael Jackson 1987

CHAPTER ONE

Erica and Dian

Erica hurried to the back end of the cafe. She wanted to grab the one remaining table in the alcove. It was just before one thirty, an ideal time, she decided, with a certain degree of self-congratulation. Still noisy enough to retain a little atmosphere but not too crowded to preclude private conversation.

They often met at The Tea Shop. Both were amused by the ridiculous comic book wallpaper in the toilets and the mismatch of bone china and leaky stainless steel teapots. Glancing at her watch she saw there was at least ten minutes before Dian was due to turn up. Enough time to look and see if their favourite Portuguese tartlets featured on the menu.

Their usual day was a Thursday, but Dian had seemed really anxious to bring their lunch date forward. Erica wondered if there was more depressing news on the mother-in-law front. Being no stranger to the disconcerting phenomena of aging parents, she was prepared to sympathise. Catching a glimpse of her rapidly greying hair in the incongruously grand gilt-edged mirror opposite was sobering. A reminder that she too was treading the well-worn path to older age: such a thought certainly merited a Portuguese tartlet or two!

Lunch was nearly over and Erica was beginning to think she must have been mistaken about Dian's urgency for a chat. They had covered the usual newsworthy items: aging parents, pending retirements of mutual colleagues, planned holidays and other events, when Dian suddenly blurted:

"Lecce has really finished with me, you know," giving a small mirthless laugh. "I sound just like a teenager, don't I?"

Erica, surprised, began to form a diplomatic reply. Knowing that whilst she had accepted, and perhaps, at a push, even understood her friend's involvement with Lecce, privately she had never really approved.

"Has she gone back to Grace?" Erica immediately realised she had been unable to prevent the question from sounding just a little too hopeful.

Dian shook her head. A single fat teardrop fell onto the embroidered tablecloth. This was not the Dian she knew. "Oh, I'm sorry. Why? What's happened – has William ..." taken unawares she trailed off. Damn, that's both feet in it!

Dian was hunting through her cluttered handbag and did not appear to notice Erica's less than tactful response. Instead, her mind was busy asking whether she should reveal her worse fears, especially to Erica. She was torn with an overwhelming need to confide in her friend but knew that Lecce would never forgive her this indiscretion.

Dian shrugged, wiping her eyes, "I suppose it's the usual. She's probably fed up with my married life and then Andrew just called out of the blue! I soon realised he was well and truly in the past. But, it's too late. I think she could be moving on to ..." Dian desperately struggled to avoid another cliché and gave up, "... to pastures new."

Erica had an unexpected and unpleasant insight. She remembered Lecce and a young woman, sitting together on the garden bench, laughing. The blond heads close together, a hand touching Lecce's arm, and, oh yes, they were whispering in what, with the benefit of hindsight, was a rather intimate way.

She thought too, that Lecce had seemed rather distracted lately, and asked carefully,

"So, you think she may be seeing someone else?"

"She hasn't said as much, but I think there might be some other interest, anyway." Dian's slow burn of distress abruptly boiled over as she experienced a flush of real indignation. "And now I sound like a wife!"

There was a pause as Dian wiped her eyes again, and gave up thinking about discretion.

"I think it's someone from work. And, what's more, I don't think this someone is making her happy. If she was happy, I could accept it. Or I think I could. But she isn't. She's distracted and peaky and thin. It's impossible to talk to her!"

Erica, guiltily relieved to be sat in their discreet alcove, poured more tea and waited until Dian was calmer before she said evenly, "Well, that *would be* ill-advised of Lecce, certainly."

Apart from that, there was very little else of comfort she could think of to say. For a while they carried on a halting conversation about nothing in particular until finally Erica had to leave.

On her slow walk back to the college, Erica gave thanks in her heart that her own marriage was a long and happy one. It was filled with peaceful companionship, children and grandchildren. Dian's marriage was so unlike her own; it was just as long but, she guessed, had been one of disappointment and loneliness.

Uncomfortably, she considered the depth of feeling and upset Dian had displayed. Her friend was so usually composed and always appeared to meet "life's little reversals" as she called them, with a pragmatic shrug and a witty aside. Erica felt a regretful twinge of chagrin; why had she never given Dian and Lecce's relationship the serious consideration it evidently merited? Had she preferred to believe Dian's airy assurances that it was "more of a loving friendship than anything else."?

As she turned into the car park she gave herself an exasperated mental shake. This was not the time to re-evaluate her views of same sex couples or extra-marital liaisons. Her friend had presented her with a thorny problem. Should she raise this with Lecce? That would mean breaking Dian's confidence. Karin Pedersen! That flaky girl! Has Lecce lost her mind!

Lecce

Lecce was glad to see the back of the Summer School. That final week had been uncomfortable and fraught beyond belief. Karin and she seemed to have come to an unspoken agreement to avoid each other. Lecce knew she should have made more effort, she should have taken the lead and tried to defuse the situation. Yet somehow that distant nod of Karin's and that briefest of thin smiles had put Lecce in mind of the way she had studied that unapproachable back curled up in the backseat of her car.

Today though, she had decided to put all of that behind her and enjoy her first day working alone in the big old ramshackle building. An afternoon of visiting every room, listing repairs and making inventories of tables, chairs, whiteboards, textbooks, cupboards, or the lack of those things had, in a strange way, enabled her to reclaim her workspace and banish all those confused feelings of embarrassment and disconnect.

The familiar smells of floor polish and whiteboard cleaner, the creaking of wood wormed floorboards underfoot and the indifferent results of Billy's efforts to clean the draughty sash-corded windows reassured her that she was once again, in control of her life.

As she walked across the freshly mown grass towards her car, she observed how large and empty the car park appeared without the endless parade of cram-packed vehicles. Amused, she thought of those fascinating photographs hanging in reception of young Edwardian ladies attempting to play tennis in ridiculously inappropriate clothing.

The box under her arm was proving awkward and heavy. It was full of tutor contracts which she had painstakingly completed throughout the morning. They were all correctly addressed and stamped, and she planned to post them on her way to meet Grace. As she lifted the boot and placed the post inside, she breathed in gratefully. Grace and she had, at last, begun to work on a tentative friendship. She was looking forward to their trip to the esplanade where Ruby Red Dog was allowed to run the length and breadth of the cobbled beach and put her hot paws into the incoming tide.

As she opened her door and made to climb into the driving seat, she was startled by the abrupt half toot of a car horn from behind. Lecce turned, perturbed as an unfamiliar small grey car she had failed to notice, pulled away from a far-off shaded corner and drew up next to her own.

As the engine abruptly cut off and a frosted darkened window slid silent down she felt a dart of apprehension and looked round, hoping to see Billy or at least his bike chained to the railings. With the high stone walls and the dense canopy of long ago planted trees, it was eerily quiet, as if the teeming life of the inner city was far more than only a few yards away.

When Karin leaned out of the window and called a greeting, Lecce was unsure whether to feel relieved or not. As she slowly walked across, she could see that last week's dreaded pallid face had filled out a little and had more colour. In fact, as she got closer she could see that there was now a fetching sprinkle of freckles across the bridge of her nose and she was smiling broadly, looking rather like the other, almost forgotten, friendly Karin.

Lecce's own smile was wary and tentative, "Well, hello! I've just locked up the building, I'm afraid." She knew she sounded awkward: formal and hopelessly managerial.

Karin's smile grew wider, "That's ok. I was picking up the new car and thought I would drop by and show her off. What do you think?"

Lecce knew very little about cars, as long as they worked and were any colour but red she was happy. To her eyes this was a perfectly ordinary three-door except for those impenetrable, slightly sinister looking windows. However, Karin looked so youthfully pleased and proud that she ventured politely, "It looks good, but can you really see out of those windows?"

Karin gave a low laugh. "Where we live, it's better if people can't look in and see what you've got." She gave the dashboard a loving pat. "And it has something any car thief might take a fancy to. Come on in and have a look."

As the passenger door swung open and Lecce hesitated, Karin brandished a disc through the window. "It's got a C.D. player and I've got a new record I think you'll like!"

Lecce was disarmed and intrigued. Her tape player constantly chewed up all her favourite music ***and*** it was important to get back on a friendly footing with Karin. Undecided, she looked at her watch and mentioned her arrangement with Grace.

"Oh, by the way," said Karin, ignoring the excuse and pointing at Lecce's car, "Did I see you put our contracts in there? Perhaps you could give me mine and save yourself the trouble of posting it."

Lecce coloured. Did Karin have second sight or something? How could she possibly have guessed what was in the box or the way she had hesitated over the completion of hers? All those unexplained absences had merited a referral to Erica. She had struggled with her conscience asking herself whether she really had only been trying to be fair-minded. Or if there was even a remote possibility that she had hesitated in case Karin might think she was trying to get rid of her?

Lecce turned back to her own car, and fumbled for the key to the boot. Swinging it up she leant in and clumsily sorted through the mail, feeling awkward and guilty. With a slow step she returned to Karin's window and handed her the package which was quickly taken but then thrown casually over to the back seat without a word of thanks.

"Oh, come on in for a minute. Let me show off my new plaything!" Karin's impatient gesture was belied by that rare and winning smile of hers.

Lecce reluctantly made her way round to the vacant seat, trying to suppress vague disquieting thoughts of keeping the door open and one foot on the ground, like they did in those old Hollywood movies. Her fervent thoughts were busy and muddled, wishing away this unforeseen appearance of even a happy, friendly Karin.

For a few minutes, Karin enthusiastically demonstrated the player in some detail. Sliding in the disc, ejecting the disc, fast forwarding, pausing and repeating a particular song until Lecce's own polite smile slowly turned into an amused grin. How like Sal and Keith this only slightly older twenty-something person was being. She looked so young and fresh in her summer coloured V-neck top and matching, skimpy, above the knee skirt. A far cry from those sober cover-up jeans and sweaters she must reserve exclusively for work. It was just too hard not to warm to her. She found herself relaxing into their old jokey banter, as if the fraught interlude of last week had never happened.

Later, whenever she tried to piece together what had happened, her mind became a splintered blurry fog of disconnected happenings. One minute they were sitting side by side examining the workings of the player and then the next, Karin had suddenly leant forwards reaching across and pushing back her seat, jerking it downwards. Lecce, finding herself flat on her back, had let out a surprised laugh; convinced Karin had played some kind of joke.

"Very funny! How do you get this thing up again?" she had said, still laughing, her hand searching blindly for the upright lever.

"You don't really want to do that, you know," Karin's, voice was suddenly mocking and quiet, almost as if she was speaking to herself. Her eyes seemed to smoke or spark as they locked onto her own and the face staring down was the other Karin, the one from the café, hard, ageless and knowing. She weakly raised a hand and began a confused protest.

Karin shook her head, her blond fringe hiding her eyes. "Oh, come on. I know you want this as much as I do." With one swift, agile movement, she had rolled across, quickly moulding her firm, surprisingly muscular torso into Lecce's own, pinning her down, and imprisoning her completely. Lecce half formed the thought, "How could anyone so slight do this?" before becoming vibrantly aware of the small rounded breasts on her own and the shock of the rush of desire as the slim hipped hardness of a pubic bone crushed her deeper into the seat and deeper still into an acquiescence she could not, and increasingly did not, want to resist.

Lecce gasped, as Karin took her hand pushed it beneath the soft cotton top. She made one last feeble effort to pull away, even as she caressed the small bare high breast and her mouth opened to accept the insistent tongue that with a delicious circling motion, expertly shut down all resistance.

With every kiss and every touch she slipped further and further down into a spiral of irrepressible desire. Her sensible self was brushed aside it seemed, as easily as her clothing. Surprisingly strong slim fingers began to seek out the no longer secret places between her thighs, probing, finding the wetness they wanted, sliding slowly inside, then quickening, pushing deeper, opening her up, melting her until she began to groan with a quickening need towards a stunned and fiery, screaming release.

"My goodness!" Karin said, lifting her head and staring down. "You certainly wanted that, didn't you?"

"I don't know. I must have done!" Lecce stuttered, her eyes slow to regain their focus and her ragged breath continuing for a further long moment. At last she became fully aware of their surroundings, realising the music had paused and in its place was evening birdsong, not too distant voices, the rumble of passing traffic, a faint breeze from the half-opened window.

"It was down," Lecce said, suddenly realising why she could hear those outside sounds with such clarity. "You left the window down. Oh god, we should never have –"Her eyes filled with horrified tears as she struggled sit upright.

"Don't!" Karin's tone held a hint of anger as she roughly pulled the seat upright, but then it softened as she moved closer, straddling her, wiping away an escaped tear with a finger. "It was wonderful, just wonderful. Don't worry, I kissed most of your screams, and my how you screamed my name! Lecce Connor, I knew you would be one sexy woman!"

Karin lightly kissed her lips before drawing the window to a silent close. "There," she said, "Is that better?"

Lecce nodded gratefully, but the new silence only served to heighten her awareness of warm breath on her face; the faint fragrance of freshly washed hair; the lean thighs across her own, those small ovals of breasts almost, but not quite touching hers. Eventually she said, realising her voice sounded oddly small and diminished,

"We should never have done this Karin."

Oh, listen," Karin shook her head in mock reproof. "That's hardly complimentary is it? Don't you know yet that this is meant to be!" she entwined their fingers in such a strong grip that Lecce winced. "Of course, we should have done that. Why not? Doesn't everything in this old world feel like it will come right after all to you, now – because it does to me!"

Lecce could not help but feel moved by this breathless little speech. What odd old-fashioned English Karin often used. She examined the smoky hungry eyes and the slight tremble of her full lips. How could this nymph, this sprite, this child-woman, want her?

Yet, it seemed as if she did, and so, both dismayed and elated she pulled Karin towards her. Kissing her hard on the mouth she let her hands slip beneath the short skirt. The car was an opaque dark and light and now strangely empty of sound. There was a faint sweet salt smell of sex and something else, something like flowers or citrus or oily herbs that she could not place, but recognised from somewhere. But soon her senses were involved with nothing more than an overwhelming need, a rampant wanting to discover the soft silken enigma that was Karin.

A wistful hope, which even then she knew to be madness, drifted across her mind: Could this, wherever they were, whatever it was, turn out to be good and true. A lucky accident … maybe …

★★★

Karin

Karin left the car park first but did not go far. She drove straight into the derelict petrol station, and parked behind the obsolete dispensers, pulling up onto the cracked tarmac amongst a scruffy collection of tall urban weeds. She frowned as she heard her pristine tyres crunch onto piled up litter, hoping there were no discarded nails or glass. She hurried to close the window against a distinct rancid smell of thrown aside half-eaten fast food. Why did something new always end up so un-new so quickly? Why did it happen with everything: things and people?

It amazed her the way the wide grey-black windscreen gave her a perfect view onto the road: the feeling of being able to watch unseen gave her such a buzz.

Five minutes went by and there was still no sign of the small blue car. She had not yet decided whether to follow Lecce or not. It would be handy to know where she was living now she was hardly ever at Dian's place. Karin glanced at her watch. Plenty of time; Jack would still be at his mother's.

She was certainly taking her time getting herself together. Well, it *was* a real sexy session and had lived up to some of her expectations. She opened the glove compartment and hunted for the small tin that held her hand-rolled cigarettes and lighter. She had almost forgotten how exciting and powerfully in control, sex with someone new always made her feel. Somehow it grounded her and submerged all those ceaseless fears and night terrors: for a while, anyway.

She had known long ago, that she was different. She was unique, just a lone wolf personality, not the misfit as her family insisted. It was only part of her that was like today. Most other people seemed to be only one-dimensional – that part she gave to Jack. Her way of hiding in plain sight – her lips twisted into a thin smile as she took a deep pull of her smoke – just like these frosted windows in fact!

Karin frowned, relighting her smoke impatiently, winding down the window a fraction. At least Jack was someone to live with, and she just could not live alone, had never been able to and never would.

After last time, she had promised Jack there would not be any other men. Well, Lecce was definitely not another man! For a moment she relaxed, inhaling the bitter acrid taste of her smoke and thought about the weird excitement of touching someone who felt exactly like herself. It was a bit like a new kind of self love. She had needed what had happened just now. She sighed, feeling the danger of her mood slipping back into that dark and dreary place where she and Jack seemed to live these days.

For a few seconds she distracted herself with her new player; using the arrow buttons until she found the track that she had put on repeat when they had been together. Through blue veined, pale, lowered lids she pictured all that crazy sex. Lecce had been completely at her mercy.

Just thinking about her screams was such a turn on! This sex though, if you could call it real sex that is, had no worries with pregnancy. Perhaps lesbian sex should be renamed safe sex! Whatever, it had been mind blowing. That was the first organism she hadn't faked for quite a while!

When Lecce finally emerged from the car park, Karin could see her clearly, even from her hiding place between the battered fuel pumps: she loved this car! Lecce looking flushed and distracted seemed to fumble with the indicator before turning into the road. So Lecce Connor was not so high and mighty after all!

The illuminated dashboard clock flicked to seven. Too late to follow her now but it would be easy to get her address. Karin twisted the ignition, her mind already forming the opening sentence of the kind of letter Lecce would not dream of ignoring this time.

★★★

Lecce

Lecce soon found herself struggling to remain composed on the short drive home. She had completely forgotten her arrangement with Grace. It was as if her heightened state was affecting not only the racing tempo of her thoughts but also her physical reactions. Her right foot had a will of its own, continually pressing too firmly on the accelerator, causing a jerky fast-slow progress along the short stretch of the motorway and only increasing her sense of agitated panic.

Suddenly, she realised that she had missed her usual turning. She had not even seen the huge black and white sign post with the long left hand turn arrow. For a second time, she made an almost emergency stop at a red light, narrowly avoiding an ominous flash from the square yellow box above.

At the earliest opportunity Lecce pulled over onto the hard shoulder, breathing deeply, thankfully cutting the engine. She pressed a hand against her bruised mouth and attempted to still the internal clamour inside her head. She rolled down her window, hoping for more air. There was the rushing noise of passing traffic and then, the babble of yet another scrambled tape. Absently, she pushed the stop button and leaned back onto the head rest.

Had all her senses gone into overdrive? Was there really a lingering sweet-bitter taste of kisses on her tongue, were her fingers still within the soft intimate folds of Karin's sex? Moving her hand away she noticed a ring of blue-black fingerprint marks around her wrist. A glance into the rear view mirror revealed a small bloody cut on her bottom lip.

Determinedly, she pushed away a fleeting flash of disquiet. They had been in a small confined space and their love making had become wild and intense. These marks were accidents only. Did Karin have anything similar that she would, obviously, have to hide from Jack? That thought brought her up sharply.

She felt a spurt of guilty shame that soon erased all the remains of the afterglow of sexual elation. Their actions had led them to betray other people, their work place and themselves. Karin and Jack were going away tomorrow. They were driving the new car, *their* new car, all the way to see her family.

Jack, whom she hardly knew but had thought of as a decent man, would unknowingly be crossing continents in the same vehicle where she and Karin's betrayal would surely still linger. He would even, maybe, sit in the same seat where she had given her whole self to the woman he believed was his.

What had happened between them had been unexpected and overwhelming. She had not seemed able to help herself. ***This could not happen again. It must not happen again.***

JACK

Jack returned to the front window and hopefully searched the downward slope of their road. Karin was late. There was still no sign of their new car. It was past eight thirty and she had promised to be home by six. A sanguine late summer day had surprisingly become gloomy. Could she see clearly in all this?

A faint drizzle was just beginning to turn into more of a sideways, slanting downpour. He did not trust those windows.

He went back to the tiny galley kitchen and examined the table layout. Was the cutlery the ones she liked or the cheap everyday ones? He picked up a spoon and saw it was stained underneath, would she notice? Well, he had better change it anyway. He wanted tonight's meal to mend the stony silences of the last few days.

The clock now showed eight forty, almost dusk, and still no promising beam of headlights turning into their cul-de-sac, no sound of a key in the lock. Perhaps the bridge was slow in crossing. It was windy. Should he turn down the chilli, or off?

Jack, felt a fleeting wave of apprehension which he firmly thrust aside. Everything had been more or less calm this year. Karin usually came home on time and seemed less distracted. She had even brought him his favourite Green and Black chocolate once or twice, and had left him an unexpected loving note on the fridge this morning, reminding him to pick up the laundry.

As he watched the clock tick off five more slow minutes, he could not shift a vague premonition that this peaceful phase was coming to an end once more. Karin had taken out her pencil case of green ink pens. This week, and last, he had come in from the garden to see, with a sinking heart, that the waste basket was full. Oblivious to his presence, she was engrossed in covering pages of unlined paper in that unnerving, uneven erratic scrawl.

He sighed as his glance fell onto the letter next to the sideboard. Another rejection, another job he had failed to get. When had he become so useless? Every time he was invited for an interview his head would start on its negative refrain: "You won't get it. You're no good at that kind of thing. "

Was it only six years since he had been promoted to Head of Department? And already five years since they had left all that behind so that they could build a life together? Then he had still felt young and vigorous and supremely confident that his time had arrived, that everything had fallen neatly into place before and would do so again: now he had somehow, some way, won Karin.

In those days though, he could afford better clothes. Jack felt frustration rise as he caught sight of his frayed cuffs and ran his hands through his hair. It had definitely receded even further lately.

Was it really such a long time ago since he had first met her? He still had the congratulations card Karin, whom he had hardly known then, had given him when he had stepped outside his new office door. He remembered flushing like a schoolboy as he had read the charming message, written in an idiosyncratic green hand:

Professor Jack Delacroix!
I knew you would do it!
You are soooo great!
You are the chosen one!

Well, there would be no congratulations tonight. He screwed today's letter into a tight ball, stuffing it into his trouser pocket. The summer holidays had been wretched for both of them until now. Thank God, they were going away tomorrow. There was the ferry and then the long, tedious journey through France, but at least that would be a distraction away from his constant failure to get any worthwhile work.

Karin had been upset when the last post had brought nothing but two more rejection slips for jobs: the kind of positions even an undergraduate should have walked into. He could still feel the swingeing stab in his bones whenever he thought of the way Karin had flung the groceries onto the table. She had run up the stairs away from him, calling down in a tone laden with disdain that he was "ineffectual", and had demanded whether she "was going to have to keep them both for the rest of her days", before slamming the door hard enough for it to rattle on its hinges.

How could he blame her for being so disappointed in him? They had both hoped for so much more from a life together, once the dust had settled. If only he could get a decent job. Apart from Karin's wage and his ever-diminishing supply work, they had nothing else coming in. "Get a grip Jack!" he told himself. "She's still with you, isn't she? At least, for this one evening, think of yourself as the knight in shining armour she used to say you were."

He went swiftly back to the window and squinted through the rain-sodden night. At last there was an orange flicker from a car indicating left. Relief washed over him as he saw the small grey fiat with its chilling blank windows, slow to the space in front of the house and in a moment the door opened on her long legs and bright t-shirt.

These years of their up and down life had not dampened that pleased jolt of utter pleasure he experienced whenever he saw her lanky youthful frame as it was now, illuminated in a halo of white fluorescent street-lighting, striding up their path towards him.

Jack picked up the umbrella and hurried to the hallway***. He was still one lucky man, the chosen one!***

CHAPTER TWO

Lecce and Karin

The only vacant room was on the first floor. It was small and shabby and overheated by a radiator that, whatever the season, refused to turn off. Its best view was of the car park, the one place Lecce did not want to revisit, even through a window. For a moment she hesitated, contemplating whether it was possible to go back down to their office. How hard could it be just to ignore the quizzical gaze her increasing paranoia had picked up from Erica this morning? And not just this morning either.

Eventually deciding that this room and this view, was the least of the two evils, she dumped her pile of exam results and the old-fashioned calculator on a middle desk before resolutely closing the broken blind as far as it would allow. It was much too warm to shut the door and anyway, perhaps those familiar and normal classroom sounds drifting across the hallway – sporadic high voices, crumpling paper and the occasional squeak of chalk on board – would soothe away all the petty irritations that had made up her day so far.

As she settled to her task she slowly became absorbed by the complexity of why a single point ended up as either a pass or fail. Figures had never really been her thing but somehow, miraculously, her calculations appeared to be revealing patterns and making sense. That minor achievement began to give back a little control over her working self which had been eroding into nothingness all week long.

For over two hours she had almost managed to shut the door on an anxiety-wracked disquiet which had implacably crept across from the edges of her mind since Sunday afternoon. She worked on towards three o' clock with a fevered determination, rapidly tapping at the keys and tearing off the printed results before pinning them together with a decisive snap.

Thankfully, the ancient adding machine finally stalled and the stapler emptied. Yet, as soon as Lecce sat back and stretched, trying to loosen a tight knot at the top of her spine, all her nagging doubts and questionings returned. Had she managed to disguise the dismay she had felt when once again Karin's name was on the absent list? Was her pantomime of mutterings enough to convince the eagle eye and ear of Rose?

She had immediately busied herself with finding a replacement and had successfully sweet-talked Marie into covering those classes again. Her jokey quips about tardy tutors though, had not stopped her heart from dropping a little more or another sharp twinge of guilty alarm from taking a firmer grip, squeezing her nerves ever nearer to breaking point.

The letters were in her bag, just beneath her feet, where she had put them on Monday morning. The mere sight of the airmail blue and red stripe and the green print of her name, half hidden beneath the disorder of a fortnight's junk mail, was all it had taken to light a flare of alarm whose heat was growing with each passing day.

There was no need for Lecce to reread them again; she already knew every word of every line by heart. Taking them from her bag, she stared down at the untidy but confident lettering. How had Karin known where she lived? Surely that information was only listed in the post book which Jenny kept safely in her top drawer. Why *did* she find Karin knowing her address so unnerving, why did it feel so – she searched for the word – insinuating?

One was more of a note than a letter and Lecce had, at first anyway, smiled at the excitable scribbled compliments. She had found them endearing and childlike. It was impossible not be flattered by the effusive title of: "Charming, Sexy, Devil-Woman." She had been intrigued and touched by the enclosed small tin tightly wrapped in elastic bands. The contents, black, volcanic sand, apparently from Karin's coastal home town, were obviously meant as a love token. Karin had actually called it "a little part of me".

Opening the tin and tentatively touching the sand with a forefinger, she worried now over the lines "because you must know I am only made of sand" rather than the romance of the gesture. The postmarks were indistinct but what was most likely the second contained a series of majestic but rather gloomy postcards by Turner. Each of the half dozen depictions of roiling seas, drowning and shipwrecks had a printed message on the back; a brief green inked description of whatever she and Jack had done for the day: a museum visit; a tea party; a hike across cliffs.

The pictures and the oddly aloof factual accounts had made her instantly uncomfortable and more than a little annoyed. It had seemed wrong somehow. It was almost as if Karin had deliberately turned her into a snooping voyeur of the private life she shared with Jack. They had left her feeling strangely shabby and, she acknowledged reluctantly, something else – jealous.

And now Karin was away. All those heightened emotions she had optimistically hoped to lay to rest by a sensible grown up discussion and, obviously, a calling of time on their ill-advised coming together, were ramped up by this inexplicable disappearance.

Her bad temper would soon be noticed unless she could get a grip: how had she let this happen? Was she having some kind of midlife crisis? Lecce stood up, dropping the letters into her bag, deciding not to probe or brood further. She would be just in time to get to the staff room whilst it was still empty. She should make tea and amends for snapping at Jenny just because her desk in reception had been taken over by an impromptu stock take.

The phone box on the wall opposite suddenly came to life. The shrill repeat of the ringtone echoed in the quiet passage, cutting through all the hum of muted activity from behind the other closed doors. Lecce froze, this was a private number, its use was intended for weekend emergencies only. She hurried across to shut down its piercing call, each nerve end on high alert, fearful that it should and should not be, Karin.

There was a brief hiatus as Lecce heard the dull drop of coins, a momentary static as the connection was complete and then, "It's me."

Lecce closed her eyes and leaned into the box, holding onto the receiver with a shaking hand. "Karin," she said, trying to disguise the weakness of her relief, "Where are you? What's happened? Are you alright?"

In the ensuing pause that followed she could hear the far-off sounds of a busy road and closer, the repeat swing and buzz of a shop door. It could be anywhere. Was she even in Britain?

"I'm alright, I suppose."

Lecce could hear Karin begin an agitated drum of her fingertips against the receiver and a scrape of a sole along the rough cement of the floor. She attempted to decipher the tone of Karin's reply. Was it sullen – angry – upset? Her own children had never been this difficult to comprehend.

With a sudden stab of clarity, Lecce realised that she must draw back from her need to keep hold of the innocent picture of a charming girl-woman, of the cups of tea and the garden bench. She must come to terms with that other Karin, the woman from the car park with whom she had quickly become complicit and transparent with a desire that overwhelmed. Today, there was this new Karin, one who had thoughtlessly, or deliberately, given her days and nights of nail-biting worry.

"Karin. You need to call reception on the usual line and explain the reason for your absence." With an effort she forced her voice into a cool semblance of no nonsense calm, "and I just can't stand here and try and guess why you haven't come in."

"You know why!" Karin's voice erupted across the line in a wild, whispered, scream. Instinctively Lecce jerked her head away, although the hissing tirade that followed was clear enough. "You know why I can't come in. It's all because of you, because of us. Because of what you made me want to do and I don't want to. I just don't!"

Lecce stood stock still and listened in trembling shocked silence whilst inside and all around her was mayhem. Rose was at the bottom of the stairs vigorously ringing the class dismissed bell. Doors were flung open and exuberant voices in a dozen different tongues gushed into the corridor.

As the bell continued to be rung, fifty pairs of feet clattered past her and down the wooden staircase. As Karin continued her whispered shrieking, there was nothing Lecce could do but press into the corner, hoping to remain unseen. For one brief, incredulous moment, she gaped down into the mouthpiece as if she might catch a glimpse, or a shape, of whatever disembodied thing was attempting to drown her in so much accusing, anguished rage.

CHAPTER THREE

Karin

Karin pulled to the curb but kept the engine running, furious that she had driven all this way without a plan. Annoyed with herself, she picked at the broken skin on her bottom lip, torn between checking to see if the dilapidated telephone box actually worked or simply walking up to the front door and ringing the bell.

It had not been easy to find her way. The endless and identical winding lanes with their potholes and overhanging hedges had taken forever. Vaguely envious and amused, she observed the row of overly neat gardens with their smart low brick walls and fancy iron gates. A slight sardonic smile played about her lips as she studied the mostly elderly occupants who were mowing a tidy lawn or washing already spotless windows. This safe little place was typically British she supposed: the total opposite of her home landscape with its biting winds and unpredictable, sea-swept landscape.

Karin physically flinched away from the word – home. Why had she gone back? Why did she always do that to herself? What had she thought would be waiting there for her? Viciously, she picked at the scab on her lip until the copper-iron taste of blood subdued the hard knot of fury that had driven her to scream out all her frustrations at Lecce on Thursday afternoon. She had not planned that either. She flicked distractedly at the thin bronze ring bands at her wrist, suddenly nervous. Without a plan she had no idea how to put things right between them or even if she dare risk what she needed with Jack. It had been much harder than she had thought to hide her disinterest, impossible to respond to him with even a semblance of enthusiasm.

As luck would have it, Lecce suddenly appeared from the side entrance of an unusually tall and sprawling bungalow, with a small dog on a leash. At the gate she turned away from where Karin was parked and walked down the street, head bent talking to the dog, stuffing bags into the pocket of an old sweatshirt. Karin cut the ignition but resisted the urge to get out or drive after her.

She would wait. On the way here, she had passed a square patch of grassy field and a playground. It was probably where Lecce was headed. As Karin watched the retreating figure, the ghost of her old confidence began to return. She would bet that Lecce was not the type that liked to be caught out in old clothes! She was always so smart at work, even her jeans were neatly pressed! Her jackets always matched and her shoes highly polished. Even in her old cut-offs she looked damn sexy though. Briefly, she imagined her hands moving up those jean shorts and finding that delicious soft wet place which had lurked at the back of her mind, keeping her distracted all through that awful, ghastly holiday.

Impatiently, she brushed the image away and opened her glove compartment taking out a small spiral-bound notebook with a miniature pen attached. She drew two thin, blank elongated faces. In the first, she fashioned a pair of downcast eyes with a single oval tear beneath each one, adding a sad mouth with a speech bubble: "Oh no! I just can't fuck my life up again!" Karin paused, tapping the pen against her teeth, her own face fixed in a pose of absolute concentration. Finally, she quickly completed the other with a suggestively raised eyebrow and a wicked lopsided grin, plus the caption: "But I'm still gagging for it!"

Looking up and through her shaded windscreen she could just make out the distant figure of Lecce and her dog on their way back. Hurriedly, she printed two words in bold green capitals.

Then she tore off the page and stuffed it into her back pocket. She hopped out of the car, locked up and crossed to the local shop, calculating how long it would take Lecce to arrive at her garden gate.

Lecce

Lecce took her time at the fields, trying to find her usual pleasure in the stroll through the late summer meadow. The weekend had hung about her, long and lonely. Guiltily she owned her parents were not unaware of the way she had deliberately avoided spending much time with them. She had turned down all their well-intentioned offers of lunches, walks or visits to garden centres, and had instead wandered morosely around the apartment or had taken Scruff out so often that even he was becoming a reluctant companion.

She missed her children, who were no longer children. She missed Ruby Red Dog and their walks through woods and sand dunes. The long lazy weekends she and Grace had always enjoyed together. She missed her old life, but somehow could not see a way back to it, not now. Grace had at least understood her attraction to Dian, but for Karin? She winced as she pictured her former partner's expression if she were ever to find out what had happened in that car park with a junior member of staff. It was the kind of uncomfortable secret she would just have to keep from everybody, especially Grace.

Once again, she toyed with the idea of finding a place of her own but that seemed so final. She still had most of the money her grandparents had left her, and at long last was well paid. She gave a little shiver as she considered the awful consequences if she and Karin had been caught. For the hundredth time she asked herself why had she done something so out of character? It had been so unprofessional, so reckless, yet so breathtakingly compelling!

Just as she reached the gate and had taken Scruff off his lead a long low whistle caused her to snap her head up and turn in surprise.

She sensed, even before she had fully taken in the figure emerging from the grey car, that the long black clad legs and the crisp red cotton shirt belonged to Karin.

"Well, hello Ms Connor! I've come a long way to see you, so I hope you're going to invite me in." Karin flourished a brightly plastic-wrapped bunch of cut flowers, which Lecce recognised as those from the buckets outside her local shop. Momentarily, she experienced a furious flash of anger. How could she just stand there smiling, holding shop bought flowers, as if that worrying week and then that telephone call was just a figment of her imagination?

There was a brief pause, before she held out a reluctant hand to accept the gift. She hid her annoyance by turning to the front door, where the dog, impatient to get in, had begun to whine and scratch at her father's flawless paintwork.

Lecce covertly examined her tall, smartly dressed visitor, and then down at her own faded sweatshirt and frayed knee length shorts. An inexplicable self-consciousness with her stature and careless shabby clothes caused her anger to abruptly fade.

"You had better come in," Lecce said, with an awkward politeness. She hurried Karin through the twin doorways and into her living space, praying that her mother would be too busy with Scruff's arrival and that her father was still tinkering with the lawn mower in the garage.

Once safely inside, she shut the door firmly and waved a distracted hand at the sofa, busying herself with finding glasses and a carton of apple juice; apologising for having no milk to make tea. She swallowed the urge to make another apology as she eyed the piled-up breakfast things on the cluttered sink top.

Karin watched fascinated, intrigued and pleased to find that the older woman she had thought cool and sophisticated could be so easily discomposed by her sudden appearance. As they drank the juice, Lecce uneasily gripped the glass with both hands and leant against the sink, keeping the breakfast bar between them.

Eventually Karin broke the silence and said, softening her words with a charming smile.

"You know, I never imagined your place to be like this. All this old fashioned furniture is quite something!"

Lecce ignored the comment, and pushed open the side window to shift the stale atmosphere she had only just noticed. "What are you doing here?" her irritation suddenly resurfacing, "How did you find me?"

Karin shrugged, "Oh," she replied casually, "I can find anyone anywhere. It's the journalist in me." She deepened her voice, arching an eyebrow and her tone deliberately seductive, added, "There is no hiding place from me, Ms Connor!"

An irrepressible and erotic memory of their semi-naked bodies, heated and frantic in the passenger seat, hidden only by smoky, opaque glass, sent Lecce into a flush of confused embarrassment. She spun back to the sink and begun to untie the flowers, once again uncertain and wrong-footed.

"After Thursday, well, I didn't expect this," she replied slowly. Her lips trembled as the surprise of unshed tears threatened to fall," I don't know what to say to you. I am sorry, so dreadfully sorry. We should never have – I should never have …"

"No!" Karin cut her off. In a single long-legged stride, she had reached the counter and was holding out her offering with a hesitant diffident hand. "***I've*** come to apologise; to explain."

Lecce considered the younger woman whose face and voice held nothing of their former swagger. She took a long careful look at the full lips now self-deprecatingly turned down and the way the downcast eyes refused to meet her own. Finally, she put down the scissors and reached across taking the page and placing it face up on the counter.

"Well," she said a slight twitch of a smile on her lips, "I've never had a conversation like this before! I usually just sit down and do my best to talk things through."

With a finger she thoughtfully traced the jagged green dividing line that separated the portraits. How was it possible that Karin, in just a couple of casually drawn sketches, had somehow managed to inveigle her into a perfectly lucid, yet unspoken, conversation?

Those twin emotions, remorse and lust, were they not also her own? Were they not exactly what had warred within her heart and mind these past weeks? No, she had not screamed at Karin in return but inside the worry and relief, the guilt and the shame had clamoured and screamed inside. How had she responded? She had hidden behind inept, prissy, management speak!

Her eyes dropped to the writing beneath the talking heads. There, in heavily printed capital letters, were just two words "GAY PANIC."

Her lips twitched again, amused at the formal bullet-pointed phrase. In her mind she added at least a dozen exclamation marks and glanced up with the beginnings of a smile that died as a twinge of shame reminded her that, for the much younger woman, all of this was most likely new and possibly scary.

"You know what Karin," she said, decisively crossing the floor and flinging open the French doors, "I'm going to borrow some milk from my Mum. Why don't you go and sit outside by the pond and enjoy the last of the sunshine and I'll make us a cup of tea."

Lecce

Lecce spent an overly long ten minutes negotiating borrowed milk, pieces of cake and deflecting Margaret's curious questioning regarding her unexpected "*young visitor*". As she measured and sliced with a fake air of unconcern, she was actively retrieving only half-forgotten memories. There was a vivid ghost of a young woman with unruly red-black Irish curls. Misty thick-lashed bewitching green eyes she had thought she might drown in. A freckled snub nose and the wide generous mouth she had finally dared to kiss.

Sudden longing and distant disappointment flittered through her heart as the sweet taste of a first, their only kiss, brushed again against her lips, as it had twenty years earlier. Aileen.

In that one long ago glorious moment, all the jigsaw pieces missing from her incomplete self had flipped into place with a joyous fanfare without even a hint of panic! Yet for Aileen there had been only denial and the kind of panic that had led to a literal packing of bags. Aileen had not screamed through the ether at her but had baldly written her goodbyes: "I do love you, of course, but not like that and if I did I would never be brave enough to say so!"

Absently, Lecce picked up the tray, giving her startled mother a quick peck on the cheek and a thank you thrown over her shoulder. By the time she reached the French doors she realised that she was almost running towards another Aileen: one that perhaps, if she got it right this time, she would not let down or lose so completely.

***

Karin

As Karin navigated her way through the crater-ridden twisting lanes she found that the exhilarated high she had left with soon began to fade as rapidly as the early evening sun. She turned up the background music a couple of notches and determinedly pushed against that familiar dark place she had managed to smother for most of the afternoon.

She let her mind wander back into the bedroom where she had left Lecce in tangled bed sheets, still flushed and breathless. Karin gave a small complacent laugh. It had been surprisingly easy to persuade her into grandma's old bed after that little talk around the fish pond.

Aileen must be the one from the short stories in that old Anthology Lecce had once admitted to having written. The book had not been difficult to find among the listed archives of the public library. If so, Aileen had definitely been a victim of gay panic! She had disappeared over night, leaving only a letter and that bracelet, her little "piece of me." It was a good story, a bit sentimental perhaps, but had been informative, a very useful way back in for her.

She had not really misled Lecce. It was far easier to let the idea of a gay thing explain away last week. No one would understand her screwed up family or why she stuck with Jack. They were secret panics she could never share.

There was nothing to panic about with being gay, or half gay, maybe. She recalled the reflected glimpses she had caught from the mirror of their two naked selves. She had liked the way they had looked, the way they had fitted together, so sensual in their sameness.

Those amazing responses! How quickly they had heightened her own arousal to the point that she had once again been able to drop over into a rare orgasm! She took her left hand off the wheel and chewed at the side of its already scarred forefinger. There was another almost imperceptible drop in her mood. Why was it only at the beginning that she could experience that surge, that powerful urge that could induce a temporary forgetfulness?

Why was it only then that she could feel something genuine towards another person, something almost approaching love, or a little less than love?

Once she had finished with the torturous laneways she sighed, relieved to find the slip road that led to the motorway. Karin turned up the music as far as she could endure, concluding that she was going to have to be more careful this time. She needed Jack, but she wanted Lecce for now. Anyway, it did not have to go bad this time. Lecce was different. Maybe even she was different? All she had to do was to keep the excitement going but put a lid on that monster: that something, someone, who just hated her to be happy.

CHAPTER FOUR

Jack

Jack was making another desultory attempt at completing the crossword. In reality, he was just marking time, clock watching again. Eventually he threw the pen down and made no attempt to stop its rolling progress across the table and onto the floor.

It was seven o'clock. Karin had only been in for twenty minutes before she had gone out again, slamming the door in that defensive way she had whenever she wanted to avoid a discussion. He had only mentioned that there was already enough milk in the fridge.

He rubbed at his eyes. They were tired from the poor lighting. He should get a hundred watt or stronger glasses. His eyesight must be going along with all his other faculties! There were times lately when he felt old, so much older than Karin, and far older than he actually was.

Another five minutes crawled by. Jack stood up and crossed to the kettle. She was taking her time just buying milk. She had walked off, not driven, but it was only a couple of hundred yards and the road was well lit. His birthday present to her, one of those new mobile phones lay discarded face down and out of battery on the sideboard. He struggled with himself not to wonder whether she had forgotten it or had left it like that on purpose, but gave in. She had taken all the loose change from the saucer on the hall table. He had heard the slip and slide of the coins as she had emptied them into her pocket; more than enough for a pint or two of milk.

How many times had she gone out to buy milk or bread lately? How many times had she emptied the saucer into her jacket pocket? A long-suppressed pain-filled rush of suspicion flooded through him. Something was up. ***That*** something was up.

The obsessive letter writing, the trips for milk they had no use for, the early and late arrivals to and from work and now afternoons every other weekend to see unnamed friends. The pattern was a depressing exact rerun of two years ago.

His distracted mind began to list a series of likely candidates, but he could think of no one in particular. They had hardly had any time to make new friends since their move and there were precious few men in her department. There were plenty of other departments though. A desperate fear began to surface which he quickly smothered. She had promised, she had sworn it would never happen again.

He ignored the whistling kettle and instead walked away from the stove and stood under the thin yellow glow. Reaching into his inside pocket, he took out the two letters he had received on Friday, easing each one from their envelope. Looking down at the first he felt a faint stirring of hope which he tried to dampen. But still, his confidence gave another bounce when he reread the invitation to attend a shortlist interview.

Jack had no need to ask himself just why he had hesitated to tell Karin this rare piece of good news. He flinched away from the memory of countless other times when interviews had come to nothing and she had scathingly expressed no surprise. He was unable to prevent his eyes straying to the drainer where now only one mug remained of the set, the others having been swept to the floor when the last rejection had arrived. No, he would wait and see. Memorising the date and time, he carefully replaced it safely inside his jacket pocket.

Jack knew that he should view this second letter as another piece of good news but somehow all he could feel was a joyless sense of self-loathing. He was well aware that he had behaved in ways he had always thought himself incapable of. If his career was forever lost, his parents eternally embarrassed and his children grew up to despise him, there would be no one else to blame.

For a moment he lost himself in the smooth feel of expensive velum on his fingertips and admired the creamy white page. Only classy solicitors could still afford to use decent paper these days. Eleanor's father had probably paid for this, and gladly so he supposed. This was no Free Legal Aid firm of the type he would probably have to look for now that she had eventually asked for a divorce.

Once again, he had kept this news from Karin and this time he was unsure of his motive. Would she still be pleased if he were free? Once she had assured him that there was nothing on earth that would make her happier, that everything would be worth it. That all she needed was to have him and chocolate!

With a weary lift of his shoulders, he thought back to those heady days when he had been the flattered recipient of adoring notes and secret phone calls. He thought with a searing shame of how he had easily brushed aside all thoughts of any dire consequences, of being a husband and a father. When he could only think of Karin and the way they were together.

He dare not ask himself if he would do it all again. It was done now and somehow he was going to make it work. Suddenly he felt a rush of determined conviction and with a renewed sense of purpose, he climbed the dim and narrow staircase deciding he should take advantage of her continued absence to review his clothes and see what would be good enough to wear on Thursday.

The makeshift wardrobe revealed his two suits, both well past their best, a half a dozen still reasonable shirts, an odd assortment of ties slung round each one. His only other decent pair of shoes was black which would mean it would have to be the older, even more worn, grey, rather than the brown.

Taking the suit from its plastic hanger he held it against himself, hoping it looked better than he feared. The man in the mirror threw back an image he hardly recognised. The receding hairline and the way the collar of his shirt gapped wide reminded him of his father. Neither he, nor the suit, would improve with just a dry clean! He imagined this new man of Karin's as taller and broader with a whole row of expensive well-cut suits and monogrammed shirts with matching silk ties.

Jack stood staring hopelessly at his shabby reflection, feeling his brief renaissance ebbing away as he continued to scrutinize the face of his father staring back at him. The dull ache of depression began to overwhelm yet again. But something inside he had thought he had lost still tugged at him. He could give in and resign himself to failure or make a fight of it. He had a credit card: something else Karin did not know about. It was for emergencies only, but if this was not an emergency what was?

As Karin's key was heard in the lock, he shut the door on his old suits with a decided slam. He went back down the stairs almost light heartedly, resolving to go the whole hog and have a complete make-over, including getting a decent hair cut and a silk tie! He would get this job and he would keep Karin. He loved her and besides, he could not have sacrificed so much, have made so many other people unhappy for nothing. She had told him "he was the one" and he was going to make sure it stayed that way.

CHAPTER FIVE

Letter from Dian

Darling Girl,

These few lines are to thank you for all the joy you have given me. And for all the fun and laughter we have shared and to ask that we may, at least, still have such times. As friends, if that is your wish?
How can I blame you? My life must seem such a muddle (although ***it does*** make some kind of sense ***to me****). Are you joyful, sweetie? How I hope you are.*
Do you remember the tale you told me of your grandmother's mirror? Whenever you were unsure if an outfit suited or a hair style was right, she would say, "Go and look in Grandma's mirror, it never lies!"
So, dear heart, go look in the mirror and ask yourself whether your new love (as a new love I am sure there must be), suits, gives you joy. As Beatrice Olive told you, her mirror never lies!
Remember, I am here, and will always be the best of all your friends.

Dxx

Lecce

Lecce sat on the old dresser stool with her back deliberately turned away from the mirror. Deep down she knew she had no right to feel so angry at Dian's letter. Nevertheless, she vehemently folded it into a dozen tight squares, as if reducing its size could diminish the guilt inducing words of love and concern.

It was a week since they had last spoken. They had met for dinner, both aware that there would be a difficult discussion to follow.

It had been obvious that Dian had taken care to dress in the way she knew Lecce admired. The slim fit silk blue skirt matched perfectly her birthday gift of tiny lapis lazuli earrings. She was close enough to catch the delicate fragrance of Dian's favourite perfume, making it impossible not to recall the early joyful welcome she had received whenever she had buried her face between those surprisingly beautiful breasts.

Seated on their familiar window seat, its poignancy was not lost on either of them. Avoiding eye contact, they had stumbled through their awkward conversation, gazing blindly through the bay and onto the long road below. Dian was no fool and had tactfully probed and kindly questioned until Lecce had felt driven to defensive, blame-filled replies, citing husbands and ex boyfriends. She had sounded evasive and dishonest even to her own ears. She had felt cornered and resentful, had wanted to excuse her secret betrayal by laying all the causes of their failing relationship upon Dian. Was this what she had also done with Grace? Was that the kind of person she truly was?

Perhaps Grace was right when she had stated flatly that since the children had left home, she had gradually begun to live inside a bubble of her own self-absorbed universe. That anything other than what she thought she needed or desired counted for nothing?

No wonder she could not face Dian or anyone else when the truth did not bear thinking about. Her fingers resumed their abstracted folding and refolding of Dian's note. How could she have actually embarked on such a crazy clandestine affair with a woman only a little over half her age? What had made her think that it was not only possible but that there had been anything remotely sensible or sane about it?

Slowly, reluctantly, Lecce turned and leaned into the mirror and examined the pale and strained face carefully. The loss of so much weight did not suit her as she had thought. Her dejected demeanour hung about her slumped shoulders as did the now over-large jacket. There were new permanent creases between her eyebrows and around her downturned mouth that she had never noticed before. No, this was not a reflection of love, of joy. There had been many heightened emotions, too many, during these past few months. Love, on her part at least, there may have been; but no – grandma's mirror did not lie – there had been a lot less than joy.

Unconsciously her hand strayed back to her collar bone. Make-up did little to disguise the purple bluish bruise. Although it no longer stung, the wound was taking a long time to fade and the painful awareness of the cause, although it still carried with it an air of incredulity, was indelibly imprinted on her mind.

CHAPTER SIX

Lecce & Karin

(ONE WEEK EARLIER)

Lecce had volunteered for the evening shift, uncomfortably aware that Jenny's gratitude was misplaced. This quiet time before evening school meant that it was much easier to hide away from too much contact with her colleagues.

Her head was full, too full. When and why had she begun to view the world through the wrong end of a telescope? Somehow she was losing her grip on everything that she had always enjoyed about her working life. Even the most mundane of conversations were hard to follow. Her mind would drift away. Familiar voices would fade and distort, until they resembled no more than an underwater echo from a swimming pool.

As she carefully sorted through the new admission applications and stacked others for shredding, she was unable to stop herself wondering if Karin, the cause of all this disconnect, had gone home again, without even a greeting or goodbye. There had hardly been a glimpse of her in the staff room for days. Even Lecce, besotted as she knew herself to be, could no longer accept that the switch on switch off tenor of their affair was this "gay panic" Karin had so vividly implied through just a couple of drawings and a sentence!

Those casual rejections coming as they always did, so close on the heels of the most ardent of love making, always left her reeling as much as any unexpected slap in the face or sudden stab from a needle. Why did they always take her by surprise? Why was the hurt almost crippling in its intensity?

It seemed to Lecce that each day's potential for happiness now hung by a thread. Had Karin chosen to wear the earrings she had given her or were her ears ostentatiously bare? Was the small bean bag wolf, they had bought together, still across the dashboard or had it been tossed negligently onto the back seat again? A flush of shame burned as she saw herself, as she had been this morning, creeping across the car park, tempted to peer through the tinted windows in the hope of catching a glimpse of the toy. Suddenly struck by her craven, incomprehensible neediness, she had turned away at the last moment, practically running towards the back gate.

In the near silence of the drab chilly room, a rare moment of clear-sightedness forced her to question whether it was possible that Karin could be orchestrating this endless circle of passion followed, as it inevitably was, by coolness and a near invisibility.

Her heart dipped to a new low as she pictured all the seedy, half-empty car parks, lay-bys and quiet park- lands where Karin, after days of aloof silence, always easily persuaded her into grateful risky sex. It dipped again as she thought of the way Erica had sat across from her in their office today, comfortably signing letters and discussing their plans for the Summer School, oblivious of the way she and Karin had abused their shared, private space.

Lecce shuddered, belatedly aware of how cold the room had become. The winter evening had steadily grown ice-cold, a ceaseless drum of sleety, slanting rain peppered the tall un-covered windows. She tested the radiator with her fingertips and saw it was set at low. With a ghost of her old smile she turned the dial to high, speculating on how many layers of clothing Jenny must have to wear to endure these practically sub-zero temperatures.

Still unconsciously hoping to catch sight of Karin, she squinted through the grimy rain-streaked windows and onto the square of garden, dimly lit by a steady yellow-orange beam of safety lights.

As she reached for the cord to pull across the blinds, there was a sharp tap and a swing of the door. A piercing draft swept through the room and Karin, like an apparition conjured up from her fevered dreams, suddenly materialised as her flaxen head and then the rest of her slid through the half-open door.

"Alone at last!" Her voice was low; a stage whisper. She raised an eyebrow in a parody of her cartoon face before switching off the lights, and speedily moving past the counter to where Lecce stood.

Unable to prevent a weak pang of relief Lecce momentarily leant against her young lover, inhaling her familiar soapy scent, acutely aware of the small well-formed breast pressing against her shoulder, the surprisingly strong arms around her waist, the minty breath and intoxicating soft lips against her nape.

"No, Karin! Not here! Never in a million years!" Somehow she shook herself free and took a decisive half step away, her excruciating hour of self-flagellation reasserting itself. She twisted away and stretched to turn on the back-desk lighting, aware that she had spoken far more sharply than she had intended and so added,

"Have you got time to come home with me? It would be nice if I could cook you something."

"Where's the fun in that?" Karin gave a short laugh. Her longer arm reached across, flicking the switch to off. "Now don't play hard to get Ms. Connor." Her voice remained low and cool yet Lecce sensed the dangerous ice-grey sea-change in the light blue eyes, caught a spark in the dim reflected light from the window.

She threw an anxious sideways glance into the garden as the intermittent flicker of a bicycle lamp briefly swept the path leading to the entrance and tried to keep her own voice calm.

"Come on Karin. Don't let's do this. You know I want to, but not here." Lecce turned the light back on and took another half step away. "Please come home with me. Or let's just go and get a coffee across the road. Let's talk for a while. Do something normal for a change!"

"What makes you think that us, that what we do is normal?" Karin gave a shrug and took a step forward, putting a hand on her arm, "I've got Jack when I want normal" she whispered, shaking her head in mock reproof. "You know when I want something real between my legs."

In the half light Lecce started in hurt surprise, shocked at the kind of crudity she never would have expected of Karin. "What we do is normal to me," she said hotly and pushed past Karin's arm stabbing at the mains switch.

The ancient fluorescent strips first hummed and then flickered on, drenching the end half of the room in a strident pale yellow, whilst leaving the front reception in shadow. Swiftly, Karin stepped out of the light and wrestled Lecce along with her. Then with a teasing grin, she forcefully squeezed them both into the corner between the bookcase and the photocopier.

As Lecce looked up at the younger woman she became aware that this was a Karin she did not recognise. Her mind grappled sluggishly at the meaning behind those words. Karin had insulted and derided everything they had shared. Her words had not been careless but deliberate and cruel. She had demeaned her sexuality and the sexuality of all other women like herself. Where was her gay pride? Why was all she could feel was a crushing, inconsolable loss?

They stood immobile, toe to toe, deadlocked. Their faces were only inches apart, their rapid breathing audible in an eerie stillness, broken only by the slow tick of the clock. Lecce could see that Karin's playful mood had evaporated completely. Her face had paled apart from a heightened flush of anger evident by the red slashes fanning outwards along her cheekbones.

The air was now thick with a tension that seemed to radiate, the difference in their height all at once felt vast and imposing. The slight almost emaciated frame had never seemed so solid and immoveable. For the first time Lecce began to feel a knot in her stomach grow into something akin to fear.

Karin continued to stare down, her eyes unfocussed and flinty. Her fingers tightened round Lecce's wrists, bruising the delicate inside skin. Karin muttered something in a language she did not understand, roughly using her weight to pin Lecce against the bookcase before lowering her head and biting down hard into the sensitive place just below her collar bone.

Lecce gave a strangled cry, beginning to struggle in earnest until Karin abruptly backed away, her hands dropping to her sides. She stood with her head down, her blond fringe hiding her eyes, her lips twisted into a thin sarcastic line. Her left foot began an agitated scraping against the rough weave of the carpeted floor.

"Get away from me!" Lecce stared across at Karin with a puzzled, disbelief. Her heart thumped, jerky and pulsating, she held a shaking hand to her throat. "Don't you realise what you've done? You've just assaulted me!

There was a long moment as the silence lengthened. Lecce heard only the rushing blood of her own pulse. Finally, Karin shrugged, lifted her head, flicking her hair back with a negligent hand.

"Is that what you want to call it?" her tone was thick with contempt. "Well, are you going to run along and tell Erica?"

With two long strides she reached the door and wrenched it open, adding as she began to turn away, "You were far too easy for me. No challenge at all …" Then, as an afterthought: "and if I were you, I'd keep our sordid little secrets to yourself … Ms High and Mighty!"

★★★

Karin

Karin hesitated under the open porch. Jack was right about the drizzle. Faint drifts of fog mixed with rain were creeping slowly from the river and up the hill towards their estate. Perhaps she should change her excuse? He had looked at her strangely when she had said they needed milk, that sad-eyed hangdog expression beginning to form. But then he had put on his glasses and picked up the paper, suggesting that she take his umbrella. Why was he always so damn nice? It only annoyed her all the more.

She did not want to go back inside and admit that the weather was too bad or face his unspoken relief as she took off her coat. Instead, she pulled at the collar of her waterproof and determinedly strode down the path towards the late night One Stop. As she hurried downwards her fingers searched her pocket to make sure she had enough change for the milk and the telephone.

The old red box was soon dimly visible as was its occupant. She sighed and slowed. She could see the smoky curl of a cigarette and someone else pacing up and down under the shop awning.

As she reached the shop, the figure in the phone box was replaced by the other and Karin took his place under the shelter, wrinkling her nose at the stale smell of a hundred dog-ends and discarded chip papers. Why did people always throw their rubbish on the floor and leave the waste bins empty?

As she waited, impatiently jingling the assorted coins in her pocket, she contemplated whether it was worth giving Lecce a call.

Her letters had been ignored. She had apologised, hadn't she? All over a little bit of horseplay that had got out of hand. Assaulted! Why did she have to overreact like that?

Turning her back against the rain she made as if reading the ragged posters roughly taped to the window whilst her mind wandered, painting an erotic replay of their last coming together in the downstairs office. She hadn't been so damn fussy then.

She pictured the way everything from the desk, filing trays, paper clips, pens and even the telephone had gone crashing down: everything littering the floor and crunching under foot.

There had been pale shadows and animated conversations from only a few yards away behind the window. In the background there had been the occasional rattle of the door handle, feet clattering up and down the stairs and the monotone from the fallen handset: all of which had driven her responses into an urgent excess of excitement and a heated release. It had felt good. Really good!

But now it looked like Lecce was getting as bad as Jack. He had not always been so prim and proper either. Irritated, chilled and aroused, she began a rapid pacing from one end of the canopy to the other. Perhaps she should just get the milk and not bother to call? Jack was getting jumpy. Maybe she should give it a rest for a while – five more minutes.

By the time she finally made it inside the booth she was wet through. She had grown increasingly on edge with the interminable wait and so calmed herself by sorting the coins, building short towers on the flat metal shelf above the dial. Then she peered into the narrow fly-blown rectangle of glass and ran a hand through her damp hair.

For a second she caught sight of her distorted image and started into sudden recognition. Behind her hazy reflection, swimming in and out of focus were two other images: her father, her brother! Karin abruptly dropped the handset. It went into freefall as it connected. She shook away the image and backed out of the kiosk leaving it to swing in a strident futile spiral.

Forgetting to buy milk or to collect the coins still neatly stacked, oblivious to the vicious side-swipe of the sleet-ridden downpour, she blindly began fighting her way uphill. Back home: back to Jack.

CHAPTER SEVEN

Lecce

Last Day of Term

Lecce sat across from Erica, aware that every so often her boss was casting an uncertain look of irresolute indecision in her direction, as if she was teetering on the cusp of asking a delicate personal question.

She glumly imagined a cartoon speech bubble forming above the older woman's head. It was liberally peppered with asterisks, question and exclamation marks! So far Erica, whom she knew hated to pry, seemed to have decided not to ask it and the cloud thankfully floated away in an unspoken puff of smoke.

Lecce fervently wished she had the nerve to take all her bits and pieces upstairs and get out of this awkward impasse with Erica. Taking refuge behind the party box, she noisily wrapped the small gifts and prizes for Pass the Parcel. The room as usual, was overheated. Whatever the season, it exuded a dim claustrophobic climate and today, was even more suffocating than usual.

At least this was the last day of term. She glanced briefly at her watch, time was running out. Soon she would have to go into the staff room, all smiles and hearty Seasons Greetings and try and ride out whatever was waiting for her in the shape of a smoulderingly angry Karin.

Karin, strangely no longer conspicuous by her absence, was to be seen wherever Lecce found herself. Every time she crossed the hallway or landing, ran down the basement steps or ventured into the staff room, she was there: waiting with that long hard stare and tight sardonic smile. And yesterday Karin had very deliberately turned her back, sharply switching on the kettle, instantly setting off its steam-filled roar, drowning out her requests for volunteers for the party.

She had brought it all on herself, she supposed. Surely it would have been easier if she had simply returned a polite but firm reply to the first letter, or had answered the telephone instead of pulling out the connection. At the very least she should have dealt with the daily stream of yellow sticky enquiries about trivial work matters left with Jenny and Rose.

Lecce bit her lip, her mind beginning its customary shut down, its veering away from the brutality of Karin's … when Karin had … It would be easier to forgive the actual … the actual … Lecce broke away before the thought could crystallize. Even … that … could be forgiven but not the words. Not the evident contempt for her sexuality' the sneering insult of the sex they had shared. That she had thought they had shared.

From across their adjoining desks, she was aware that Erica had begun to resume her perplexed scrutiny and so picked up the box, mentally squaring her shoulders, telling herself she had a job to do. This time Karin's presence must not prevent her from going into that room and talking to her own staff.

Twenty minutes later she almost fell through the heavy office door, grateful to find that Erica had already left for her meeting. For a few moments she leaned against it, pressing its contours hard into the small of her back, searching for some strength in the pressure of its solid wooden weight.

Her desk was only a few feet away but as her knees weakened, she sank down onto one of the guest chairs. Her entire body felt liquid and fragile. Trembling, she vainly tried to control the harsh ragged sobs rising in her throat and to slow the hammering of her heart.

The crowded room had been so untidily familiar and noisily friendly and, at first glance, empty of Karin. Relieved, she had felt safe, protected, ordinary and normal. The end of term atmosphere in the crammed room was cheerful, high-spirited and hectic. They had greeted her warmly, welcomed her in as one of their own.

She had already begun her customary end of year vote of thanks and offerings of biscuits and chocolates before she had caught a glimpse of Karin. A chillingly isolated figure resolutely turned away from the room, working assiduously at the computer, apparently indifferent and untouched by her surroundings.

The rapid whispering click, click, of the keys had soon started to insinuate itself. Its rhythm relentless, keeping time with her every word until she could no longer think. Until she had faltered and then finally trailed off mid-sentence: paralysed into silence by a keyboard.

When Karin had abruptly snapped the cover closed, there was a sudden heavy quietness to the room which no one seemed willing, or able, to break. The collective gaze had then been transferred from herself and Karin to the trajectory of the chair as Karin pushed it roughly aside. It had travelled a few feet on listing wheels before colliding into the desk behind. Her pale face impassive, Karin had calmly walked out, stepping over bags and feet with exaggerated care, leaving the door swinging and creaking open on its rusty hinges.

Someone, perhaps it was Rose, had hurried forward to her rescue, taking the presents she was still holding out in shaking hands. Colour was only now returning to her face which had seemed to drain completely in one ferocious cold wave when Karin had left.

At Rose's whispered insistence she had not: "Run away from that nasty, silly girl."

Somehow, she had forced a smile and had accepted the concerned cups of tea and mince pies thrust at her from every direction. She had even managed a few wisecracks and joined in with some of the jokey banter, all the while desperately waiting until the gradual resumption of normal conversation meant that she could leave. Hide.

Above, there was the reassuring noise of a party in full swing. The scamper of feet on the wooden floor shook the office light fittings whenever there was a mad rush for the vacant chairs. The echoes of loud laughter seeped through the thin plastered ceiling. This was the first time she was not in the hilarious thick of a Christmas party. The stifling heat and the poor lighting in their office was just what she needed right now.

Lecce wrapped the room around herself and breathed in deeply, inhaling its commonplace, stale, homely air, relieved by the relative quiet, and thankful to the others for so efficiently taking over the arrangements. Had she had the presence of mind to have made a sensible reply to her perceptive friend's questions?

What had Marie said as she had flung herself down next to her? Something about who had rattled Karin's cage?

"Oh, my job is like that. It's full of rattling people's cages! Having to say things to people they don't like."

Was that what she had replied? Had it had the correct ring of casual dismissal? If only she could tell Marie. But how could she explain. What could she say? Karen was right. It was no more than a grubby, sordid secret and impossible to justify even to her best friend.

Lecce grappled with her foggy thoughts. If there was any help to be had then she would just have to find it within. She sat forward, hands compulsively twisting in her lap, staring vacantly down at an old coffee stain on the plain brown carpet. Every fibre of her being strained as it made the huge mental leap to push aside the murky stupor of these past few months.

When she had first fallen for a woman, hadn't she been frightened but also crazy in love then? Of course, she had. There had been reams of letters, phone calls, and many almost endings. But, even with Aileen, who was spooked enough to run away and marry the next man who asked her, it had never been like this. There had still been some joy, some love and kindness left between them.

So what had driven her into this kind of love affair that was capable of invading every aspect of her waking life? Her nights too had morphed into a mere half-sleep where erotic images continually paraded and danced across her dreams, startling her into a fevered wakefulness. It was madness and she had fallen headlong into it! No: this was not love. This was an irrational compulsive sickness and somehow she had become complicit, had begun to crave its insanity!

Lecce lifted her head as a gradual awareness of the slowing tempo of the party drifted down and back into her consciousness. The music had faded; much of the excited laughter was ebbing through the back entrance. From the windows she watched as small groups of students hugged their goodbyes. Others were unlocking bicycles or chatting to tutors as they helped pick up paper plates and cups from the benches.

Her parched lips began to form a slow, unfamiliar smile as her bruised heart warmed towards all that positive activity outside. She loved her job. It had taken a lot of hard work to get it. It was the only safe, sane and understandable kind of love she could be certain of. She could not, would not lose it to an insanity that had only begun when she had met Karin. That maybe ***was*** Karin.

End of Part Two

Part Three

"Who do you think you are, runn' around leaving scars: Collecting your jar of hearts. Tearing love apart"

Christina Perri 2016

CHAPTER ONE

Marie

As Marie completed her notes, she paused before returning them to Karin's tray. She took a moment to run a hand through unruly long dark hair and retied her loose pony tail. What was bothering her about today?

All three classes had been a pleasure to teach. All the students were not those reluctant A-level re-sit types she found so frustrating. Her arrival was greeted with enthusiasm and at the bell she had received quite a few gratifying compliments. Her mouth turned up in a wry smile. She had insisted that they repeat the offered plaudits in French!

One group had said she was "sympa et cool!" A tall gangly youth with the early signs of a woeful attempt at a beard had given a good impersonation of a Gallic shrug, when she had suggested that the much younger Karin must be "Encore plus cool". Another had chimed in, observing that Karin was indeed "est charmantel" when not "en colere contre eux!"

Marie knew that many students, especially if they worked nights, were tardy when it came to arriving on time and resented being reminded of their lateness. It was easy to imagine the volatile Karin not bothering to hide her annoyance. What was worrying was that each class had all made their own spontaneous comments. If pieced together, they did not reflect too well on their usual teacher.

The final group were a little older. Their third level French was much more competent. She was surprised to be thanked profusely for remaining in the room for the whole period and by being called "magnifique" simply because she had offered to mark any outstanding homework!

Flicking open an exercise book she could see many unmarked pages, or corrections without any helpful commentary. Marie groaned, exasperated. She was beginning to wish she had not volunteered to cover these particular classes as a quick check of the thirty or so others yielded the same result.

Crossing to the kitchen area she searched amongst the jumble on the tray for her peppermint tea sachets, thinking that in lieu of a large glass of Merlot they would have to deputise! Fortunately, the staff room was unusually empty and so she cranked up the radiator and luxuriously sprawled across an armchair, dumping off her work pumps, thankfully putting her feet up on an untidy pile of outdated magazines. She gave her ankles a cursory inspection. Were they a little puffier today? Perhaps she was going to have to start resting them a bit more.

As Marie sipped her tea, her thoughts returned to the puzzle of the afternoon. Perhaps all that student dissatisfaction she had picked up on was connected with that unpleasant moment in the staff room on the last day of term?

That incident had been embarrassing. For everyone it seemed, apart from Karin! But Lecce had been visibly much more than embarrassed. Marie took another sip and searched for the correct word. How had Lecce looked? Marie hesitated, finally opting for "heartbroken". Was that the only way to describe the stricken expression in her friend's eyes?

Surely she must have misunderstood? Lecce was far too level-headed, far too professional. It was ludicrous! She would never involve herself with Karin, or anyone else at work for that matter. There had been Dian, of course. But that was different.

Dian was such a charismatic and attractive personality and she had retired years earlier.

She considered the way Lecce had avoided most of the Christmas party, arriving only at the end. Even then she had been no more than a pale shadow, making obligatory holiday best wishes or taking refuge with the children from the crèche. Karin had not made any kind of appearance. She had not gone straight home though. Where had she come across her later that afternoon?

Everyone else was down stairs involved with the festivities but, as the office was closed, she had run up a floor to find some paper and coloured pencils to occupy the children. Frowning, she conjured up the memory of Karin's reaction to the lights coming on. The sudden glare had cut off the spooky gloom of the strange thin elongated shapes invading the tall walls and high ceiling from outside. She had given a start of shock as one such shadow had turned towards her as Karin moved away from the wide bay windows, making no effort to disguise her hostility.

Nevertheless, she had joined her at the alcove and tentatively suggested that she come down to the party and at least take advantage of any food still remaining. They were both of equal height and briefly their eyes had met before Karin's had slid sullenly away. With an emphatic shake of her head, Karin had attempted to pass her without replying. Marie had put a hand on her arm and had tried a more straightforward approach: "If something's bothering you Karin, would you like to talk about it?"

Karin had shaken off her hand and had slid past, almost with a push She had made no effort to hide her growing annoyance, muttering something like, "Just tell that Lecce to leave me alone, that's all." She had then scampered, childlike, down the stairs rushing through the front door at almost breakneck speed! Had she done something rather like it at a staff meeting some months earlier? Didn't a chair going flying that time, too? The girl was obviously a loose cannon, despite those charming blond good looks and the usually cool exterior.

She should have made time to seek Lecce out and probe a bit deeper. What kind of friend was she? But Lecce had put her off all over the holiday break. Had made excuses not to go shopping and had failed to turn up on Boxing Day as she had promised.

Still deep in thought, Marie found that she had broken her golden rule of washing only her own cup and flung down the tea towel in disgust but then began to scrub vigorously at the coffee stains on all the discarded spoons. Staff rooms were the same the whole world over. Stuffy rooms full of messy old magazines and dirty cutlery!

As she continued to tidy and put things away she berated herself for doing no more than just organise the party and keep everyone too busy to talk about that unpleasant little episode. When Lecce had failed to appear on Boxing Day, she should have made the effort to call round. Was pregnancy making her self-absorbed already? Why had she only just realised that she and Lecce had not really sat down together and talked as friends for weeks? No, it must be months, well before the end of the Sumer term, perhaps.

After wiping down the drainer and putting away the final spoon, she hopped awkwardly away from the sink, pulling on her winter boots. Marie decided to take the late bus instead and wondered if she could persuade Lecce to take up their old tradition of coffee on a Monday. Somehow that too had fizzled out along with their occasional evening meals or shopping expeditions. This was already the second Monday of the new term.

★★★

The following evening, as Marie prepared herself to endure an endless wait for the bus, she reviewed yesterday's stilted conversation with Lecce and struggled to quell her increasing alarm. It had been hard work to persuade Lecce to come out with her. It had been impossible to talk her into coming home for dinner so they could have had a proper chat. Instead, Lecce would walk no further than the college canteen which had given off its usual depressing air of under-heated abandonment, the machine offering nothing but collapsing plastic cups of weak and watery hot chocolate.

Marie sighed and gave a third twist of the long scarf about her neck and shoved already sheep-skinned hands into deep pockets. She peered hopefully through the flimsy Perspex panels until she finally caught sight of her bus edging its way through the rush hour traffic.

Once onboard, Marie thankfully made her way to the front end of the bus where there were two seats free, one for her and another for her overlarge bag. That was something else she was going to have to keep an eye on, no more heavy bags. Her face softened at the happy thought that the baby would be born in June, just at the start of summer.

Throughout the tedious stop start journey, her thoughts continually returned to her friend. How had it been possible not to have noticed such a marked change in Lecce before now? Surely she had lost too much weight to be healthy. What had happened to all that bounce and confidence? Instead of her usual carefree gallop across the road, Lecce had dithered in the door way and then hesitated at the curb, panicking back onto the pavement as a small grey car with impenetrable frost dark windows, spewing spray and exhaust, had hurtled past.

Lecce had pushed aside her lukewarm drink and immediately hidden behind a barricade of bright small talk, focussing exclusively on Marie and Jake's wedding plans and to speculate on suitable names for the baby. Marie had tried everything to get Lecce talking about herself but whenever she had made the attempt, Lecce's eyes would shrink and shut down and her replies became vague and evasive. All of this was so un-Lecce like.

She had tentatively broached the subject of Karin's continued absence, asking if she had any idea whether cover would be needed for the rest of the week. Lecce had started and blanched at the name and had begun an agitated circling of the salt from the split packets that lay discarded on the sticky table top.

"I've no idea. This is just what she does," she had said, her eyes downcast, fingers still making their salt circles, adding in a desperate rush of words, "Is it so very bad of me to wish that this time she would just never come back?"

As the bus made its jerky progress through the city back streets, Marie remembered how Lecce had not waited for her surprised reply. Instead she had begun to bustle about, helping her on with her coat and insisting that she should not miss the next bus. With a sinking heart, Marie had to accept that Lecce's reactions had not been those of a frustrated manager. Her tone had been sad not irritated and her reddened lids betrayed recent tears. She was holding back a secret, a secret that she did not seem able to share. A secret that involved Karin and it was hurting her.

As Marie stepped down from the bus, she arrived at her reluctant decision. She could not just react in the way she wished. She could not just be the caring and discreet close friend that could bide her time until Lecce was ready to confide. As Lecce's deputy, she had to address Karin's disruptive absences and apparent disinterest with her classes ***now***. Privately, she agreed with Lecce: a permanent absence would be the best thing for the department, and so it would appear, for Lecce. Yet, Karin was entitled to as much support as anyone else.

There was really only one other option, even if it did leave her feeling somewhat like a shabby friend. As it was unlikely that she could work with Lecce on this, she would have to take it to Erica.

CHAPTER TWO

Karin

(First day of term)

Karin stood, shivering slightly, in the shadow of the outbuildings. She was cold and her lightweight jacket was not much use for early January. She never minded the dark but it was a filthy place full of mud and litter, both of which were sticking to her only decent pair of boots. Whenever she moved even a fraction she could feel the stinking and slimy grit sliding under their thin soles. The air was putrid with clogged drains and beneath the incessant drip, drip, drip of the broken-down pipe she thought she could hear the frantic scuffle of rat life.

There was no other way she could have a clear view of the car park though and so she determined to stay put no matter how long it might take. Eventually she saw Lecce with another female figure. As they reached the edge of the grassy verge, the security light went on and bathed them for a second in its dim orange glow. Karin could see the other woman was definitely not Erica. She was wearing a flamboyant cloak-like thing, and had a protective arm around the shorter woman's shoulders. Their heads, one silver, the other blond, leaned towards each other as if in earnest conversation.

Karin bit distractedly at her bottom lip, reopening the scab that had barely healed. She had thought Dian was well and truly out of the picture. She worried at the hard outline of the figurine on a necklace beneath her sweater: Would Lecce tell Dian? Would she talk to Erica or that friend of hers – Marie?

With a shudder she retreated further into the grime-laden brick-work, oblivious to the way it rubbed against her clothing. A mean insistent voice began to nag. She squeezed her eyes shut trying to close down the hideous sounds and images that swam and rocked her mind. She retreated further into the filthy corner, clapping her hands over her ears in an effort to silence the shrill echo of familiar accusations: "Unnatural! Heartless! Monster!"

The metallic sound of slamming doors, the cough of a cold motor spluttering to life jerked her grateful senses into the present. With a decisive shake of her head, Karin flung off the remnants of her sudden panic and quickly stepped forward to watch the tail lights of Dian's car disappearing through the exit. As she listened to the engine dwindle away into the distance, she angrily kicked out at the squalid debris. Lecce was almost certainly going home to be comforted by that woman.

The wild dark fury that had simmered inside throughout the day reasserted itself. Why had Lecce gone out of her way to infuriate her this morning? Acting like the big boss woman, handing out timetables and leaving notes in her tray telling her to get Erica to endorse that application? No wonder she had lost it!

Karin bit down hard on the bleeding scab, finding relief in the sharp taste of blood on her tongue. No one had the right to treat her like that and especially not Lecce! Why did it always turn out like this? All she had wanted was for her to endorse that wretched form. There was no point asking that dithering old woman Erica, she would probably lose it on that messy desk of hers within half an hour.

There must be a way to make Lecce sign it. If they knew what she was really like, if they found out what they had got up to inside practically every room in the building! That would be the end of Ms High and Mighty!

Her light blue eyes hardened into slate-grey and her lips twisted in satisfaction as she thought of the way Lecce had cowed away from her tonight. That annoying self-assured smile and the feeble excuses had soon faded along with her expensive ski suntan!

Almost frozen to the marrow, breathing out a long stream of frosty air, she made her way from her disgusting hideout, scraping her soles on the corners of the waterlogged steps with a grimace of distaste. Stuffing her un-gloved hands into her pockets, and turning up the inadequate collar of her coat, she hurried across to the furthest end of the car park to where her car was parked half obscured behind the huge municipal wheelie bins.

She definitely needed a warmer coat and some better boots. She left on her scarf, shrugging off the ineffective jacket onto the passenger seat. Now Jack had finally got a decent job he could get them for her. It would go some way to make up for hiding his own new clothes at his parents' house before the interview!

Karin pushed away a quick dart of anger and chose to feel amused instead. At least he had shown a bit of spirit for once. It was a shame that he had spoiled the good news by puffing up his chest in that annoying way he had whenever he thought he had done something great. It was only a job after all, but still, it would mean more money coming in and less worry about bills.

Her irritation with him quickly returned. Why had he not told her about the divorce proceedings – or the credit card? He must know by now that she could always find out anything. Was it worth marrying him anyway?

Well, Lecce had turned out to be no better than the others. She had just better sign that form and keep her mouth shut! Karin smothered a brief pang of anxiety. Of course, she would keep her mouth shut. She had too much to lose.

Switching on the ignition and dialling up her music, Karin began to relax into that strange calm that always came after she finally gave in to that monster-self, that violence that was no fault of her own. That was far too beyond her control.

Careful to avoid her reflection in the rear and side view mirrors she edged through the gate and into the road, time to go home and be nice to Jack for a change. At least he understood her. She had wanted Lecce, but she did not need her. That was gone. If she needed anyone, it was probably Jack: for now anyway.

CHAPTER THREE

Jack and Karin

Jack was almost bent double with the effort to make it to the top of the incline leading to their cul-de-sac. The driving sleet and ice made heavy going for his knee, already suffering from the biting cold. Finally, on the crest he could just make out the foggy outline of their car, still stationary, still in the exact same position from the afternoon before.

His patience with Karin was already stretched to the limit. If she had decided not to go to work again, why the hell had she not just said so? It would have saved him two trains and a bus journey each way. Pushing the hall door open, he stood irresolute on the threshold and sniffed at the stale damp air like a wary dog. He massaged his temples, the sharp stabs of a headache arriving.

The kitchen was in darkness, there was nothing remotely like dinner in the oven and the only light was from the landing. He debated whether there was any point in calling out his arrival; he had slammed the door hard enough to let the neighbours know! Taking his time, he took off his coat and boots, giving his briefcase an angry shove to the side and went to search the fridge.

With a hopeful half an ear he waited for Karin's light tread on the stairs but there was only the thin sound of the six o'clock news from the adjoining wall with next door. Apart from an empty packet of crisps and a half glass of water, there was no sign that Karin had spent much time down stairs. Like the car, she was probably in the same position as when he had left her early this morning. A cold hand touched his mind as he pictured the unapproachable shape huddled under the duvet, feigning sleep, letting him leave without even a goodbye.

As he emptied the remnants of yesterday's dinner into a saucepan, wrenching open the drawer for a wooden spoon, his thoughts were a confused mixture of relief and despair. Karin like this was awful but the end always began this way. The moody hostility, a near- starvation diet and the strategic leaving of clues, were all part of a pattern he hated and hoped for in equal measure.

From his pocket he took out a crumpled photograph and a few folded envelopes. These had all been waiting for him this morning, barely concealed in the waste-bin under the hall table next to his keys. He studied the photograph, feeling the hot heat of jealousy burn at the back of his eyes. It was Karin of course, posing outside the wolf enclosure at the zoo smiling, her arms possessively around her companion's neck whose head though had been savagely cut out by one or two jagged and vicious snips. There was some satisfaction in that, he supposed, but what was left of the likeness was not the six foot two rugged male in expensive suits and flashy ties of his apprehensive imaginings.

As he studied the figure far more closely than he had had time for this morning, a foggy impression began to dawn. Even headless, it was clear that the person was much shorter than Karin. The close-fitting jeans and the open blue patterned white shirt identified the image as undeniably feminine.

Baffled, he put the photograph down and considered the envelopes which were all tantalisingly empty. The distinctive right sloping script was also definitely feminine and one he was sure he recognised. He stepped from the stove, stunned and as he made the connection it was as if an unseen hand griped his heart and squeezed.

He stood, half paralysed, with a bewildered sensation of helpless betrayal. Lecce Connor! How could she have done this to him?

He remembered his first impressions of the vibrant self-assured professional he had worked with. He had liked her. He had believed in her, he had put his trust in her. He had believed Karin was in safe hands.

The smoke alarm stuttered into a whine as the overheated pan boiled over and the stench hit his nostrils forcing his numbed mind into action. He flung open the back door, throwing the pot as far up the garden path as his full force would allow.

Jack marched the few steps through the frost bitter night and with a perverse pleasure inspected his handy work. The contents had artistically sprayed its lumpy brown contents across the newly whitewashed back wall and was already solidifying and freezing into place.

Well, who cares? He shoved his hands into his pockets and turned away. Let her see what another mess she's made!

Karin

When Jack had walked out after packing an overnight bag, Karin had remained bolt upright leaning back into the headboard, rigid with shock. She had watched at first amazed and only faintly perturbed. He seemed so out of character as he had shouted and flailed his hands around, sweeping everything from the dressing table and onto the floor. It was only when the brandy glass splintered and it cracked in his clenched fist. It was only with the sudden sight of blood dripping from an angry gash across his fingers that a slow creeping fear of abandonment opened her mouth in a gasp.

"No, Karin. Don't say anything. I'm not going to listen this time." Jack had held up his bloodied hand and stated with an unearthly calm note of finality. "You can't go through life like this. You can't have everything! Sometimes you just have to choose!" He had thrown open the wardrobe door and had begun flinging things into his bag. "You need me, Karin, you know you do, but I'm tired and I've had enough. You've got to choose and if you won't, then you can leave. No more games!

Karin gnawed at her already shredded fingers, splitting existing scabs around the skin, until the painful wounds quieted her mind enough to think. Perhaps it was a good thing he had stopped her from speaking. She had neither admitted nor denied anything and she would just need to convince him. He had taken the car so had probably gone running to his mother like before. At least that would give her time to get her story straight.

As Karin began to sort through the debris from the dresser, she tried not to panic. This time, whatever she said would have to be good. Something Jack could accept; something plausible. Tearing pages from the newspaper, she began to wrap the broken glass, pausing as an intriguing headline grabbed her attention. Even before she had finished reading the short piece, a passable explanation for Jack and a way to keep Lecce quiet at the same time had begun to play out in her mind.

Jack was right, she needed him, was just a mess without their life together. That other Karin would take over completely. She would have to choose Jack and if that meant that Lecce would be the one to drown in all this mess, then so be it. Why couldn't she have been different? What did she expect would happen?

CHAPTER FOUR

Dian

Dian watched from the window until Lecce was no more than a receding stick figure timidly, yet resolutely, turning the long curve of the road. Leaning slightly forward onto the high sill, she screwed up her eyes and squinted, wishing she could find her glasses, wanting to catch a final glimpse. Once certain that the busy morning people traffic was utterly empty of Lecce, only then could she bring herself to wander away and back towards the breakfast table.

She slumped into a chair and finally permitted her own emotions to surface, deliberately relaxing her worried mouth, grateful to ease all those tense facial muscles schooled into a calm facade ever since Lecce had come home with her. She surveyed the sad breakfast table with its boiled eggs grown cold and tea stewed in half full cups. Frustrated and uneasy, she questioned her own sanity.

What a stupid idea to dress up the table like this! As if embroidered tablecloths and bone china could recreate the memory of so many happy mornings they had spent together. As if a silver teapot and flowers on the table could mend whatever ailed her love – her darling girl, her sweet love.

Lecce had insisted on going into work again, plastering make-up over puffy lids and dark shadows, determinedly refusing a lift. Rather than the usual wordless shake of her head though, this morning, Lecce had looked up from the table and had said, with the smallest of smiles.

"No, just stay as you are. You look so lovely in that red kimono," and then, almost shyly, she had taken her hand across the table, kissing the palm, in the same old way, adding, "It will be nice to think of that on my walk in!"

Dian brushed away the pricking tears and pressed that hand to her heart. It seemed so long since Lecce had said anything remotely loving and intimate to her. When had Lecce started to lose so much weight and look so haunted and drawn around the eyes? Dian pictured the halting gait and the undecided tread of the figure on the road. Where was that confident swing, that endearing almost-swagger? What could possibly have happened – or was it who had happened?

Why would Lecce not return to her own apartment, not even for fresh clothes? For the past fortnight she had just washed and ironed the few things she had left in the spare room months ago, throwing them together without caring whether they were a match or not. It was so unlike her. Usually she was such a clothes horse! Then there was all that hand wringing beneath the table and the way she almost jumped out of her skin if the phone rang. But, much, much more disturbing, was the careful way Lecce still moved as if the cotton fabric of her shirts were painful on her skin; as if they were made of sand paper.

Dian was bone weary. She pushed her plate away and considered for a moment cancelling all her morning appointments and going back to bed. They had spent another restless night as Lecce had tossed and turned eventually creeping from the room once Dian had feigned sleep. As the light filtered through the crack in the open door she had strained her ears until there was the faint reassurance of turning pages and the scratching from a pen on paper. What was she writing in that diary? Why wouldn't she or couldn't she talk to her instead?

Dian's thoughts turned to yesterday's shopping trip with Margaret which had extended into a late lunch. Normally they both tactfully avoided any possible tricky conversations that included Lecce's private life. But Margaret, naturally enough, had wondered when her daughter would be coming home, letting the unspoken question that perhaps Dian had miraculously become free from her worn out marriage hang hopefully in the air.

Finally, Dian had felt compelled to repeat Lecce's vague excuse of "needing an early start until the new term settled". Her friend had then unexpectedly let slip, with a disapproving emphasis on the "young", that Lecce had been strangely reticent about a tall young blond woman called Karin who had made a sudden appearance late last summer.

Margaret had absently added extra sugar into her coffee and then remarked, with a bewildered shrug, "I don't know who that girl is, but she certainly likes to write letters and make late night phone calls! Even Ray has noticed how quiet Lecce has become. He says she's turned into the kind of morose teenager she never was!"

It was only now that Dian recalled where she had heard the name before. Erica had included it in an irritated list of tutors that lacked "a certain reliability" as she called it. Was it the same Karin as the tall flaxen-haired, self-effacing waif who had been collecting board markers and registers in reception when she had dropped in to say hello to Jenny and Rose some time last year?

Dian began to speculate whether her first impression may have been a false one. Had there been something knowing in the girl's downcast look as she had hurried from the room? Had that slight smile held a superior smirk as if she was keeping an amusing secret? It must have been around the same time as she and Lecce had broken off their romance. She sat on at the table leaving her toast to harden, letting the clock tick by, wanting to dismiss her disquiet as just the talk of the green-eyed monster.

Later as she fiddled with the back of a particularly difficult earring, she paused, staring abstractedly back at her own frowning reflection, absently caressing the lobe, trying to find a way through her own bruised ego and muddled self-recriminations. An insidious suspicion, a growing distrust of this Karin pestered at the back of her mind. What kind of person was she? How could such a little slip of a thing wield the kind of power that could diminish and shrink someone like her clever, her self-possessed, her irrepressible Lecce?

Dian gave a short sharp laugh. How easily she had slipped over into hyperbole, into a Frankenstein melodrama! Or had she?

Those slow careful movements when Lecce had picked at her food and attempted to drink her tea. Were they only symptoms of fatigue and upset? Had there been more than a serious argument? She had no idea that Lecce could cry so hard and yet remain so tight-lipped. What was she hiding? What had Lecce got into? Why could she not talk about it? Abandoning the earring and her half made-up face, she abruptly pushed aside the stool, upending it onto a stack of neatly ironed clothes that she had meant to put away.

She hurried down the hall, making for the spare room and flung open the door, not daring to falter or think about what she was going to do. There was a cluttered box on the chair beneath the window. When had that been brought here? Even with the curtains drawn and in the low light of a January day, she could see that it was over half full with envelopes, postcards, photographs and other paper keepsakes all held together with a large elastic band. The diary, with its tattered cut out photographs stuck to the cover, lay on top of the pile.

On impulse, her hand moved towards the diary and then away. Lecce had told her once that this was just one of many diaries, the first of which had been a gift. Her grandmother had given her it when she was fourteen, saying that, "Every woman should have somewhere to keep her 'private mind.'"

For a long, long moment, she stood with her hands clasped, poised just inches from the box. Surely to intrude into Lecce's life like this, into her private mind, would be breaking all the accepted boundaries of love and friendship in the most unforgivable of ways?

Yet perhaps, in the name of love, in the name of the truest of loves, it could be done – should be done? How else was she going to help her darling girl, her sweet, sweet love?

CHAPTER FIVE

Diary Entry

I'm looking at all these endless blank pages, all dated and ready and empty. Where has my "private mind" been all these months? I suppose I just haven't wanted to talk – even to myself. If I had, maybe none of this would have happened. Is this why Grandma believed in diaries? I wish I could ask her. I wish she was here.

I remember a quote from somewhere. It says something like "All sorrows can be borne if turned into a story". Perhaps I should start where it doesn't hurt so much. Where there can be some kindness on the page. Work my way round to the "sorrow"?

After

(two weeks earlier)

I had locked the door. When the key turned it left me open and exposed. It was Erica and as soon as she caught sight of me she dropped her bag and came and sat opposite, pulling her own chair close, taking off her glasses and smoothing down her skirt in the way she does when she's agitated. Her eyes are brown and they were bewildered and sad.

For a while she sat reassuringly silent, just passing me paper tissues, waiting for me to stop crying. My eyes were melting, just melting endless, awful, shaking sobs of stinging tears. It felt as if everything inside me was melting and not just my eyes. My blood, my bones, my heart were all melting away into a nothingness of confusion. How could I have let that happen? Did it happen?

When the phone rang, she calmly picked it up and laid it on the desk and waited. Erica is such a patient woman. I have observed her do this countless other times with staff and students and now it was me! I was too far gone to be embarrassed though. So we sat that way for a bit. I cried and she worried at imaginary specks on her skirt until she was certain we had reached an impasse.

Then she switched on the kettle and made tea. As she placed the mug in front of me, I tried to drink it but my hands were shaking too much and it slopped onto the table. I put it down and remembered with a sinking feeling another similar offering of a cup of tea.

"Why does everyone keep making me tea?" I said.

Erica carefully mopped up the spill. "Well, Lecce, if you won't tell us what's going on then all we can do is make tea."

I wanted to say something. I really did. How could I tell her? I couldn't. I can't. A hundred thoughts tumbled inside my head but nothing came out. Inside I was screaming. Speak! Speak! Speak! On the outside there were only tears and tears and tears and a stubborn, shamed silence I just could not break.

I thought of Dian. Of her gentle hands and her kind mouth and how they would never have betrayed me in such a way. And I wondered what was wrong with me. Why had I not been able to accept all that she could offer? Why had I so easily settled for so much less? And Grace, but I dare not think of Grace.

"Can you call Dian? Can you ask her to come?"

Erica, looking relieved, hurried to reconnect the phone. She made the call and Dian came in ten minutes, wrapped in her orange and brown poncho, her cheek bones high and flushed with the colour of cold or concern, looking so lovely and so familiar and so safe. It had been weeks, maybe months even, since I'd seen her. She came with not a hint of reproach in her eyes. She quickly bundled me into my coat, packed my bag and took me home without one question asked.

We sat in our alcove, on our seat where we had first kissed and I tried to tell her. But my eyes began their melting again and I only told her I was sorry. Sorry I had been so shallow and had loved her so little after all.

Later, Dian lit all our night lights and carefully placed them so that they reflected and flickered on the long narrow walls and onto the high ceiling of the bedroom. She made me smile with her shadowy rabbit and foxy hand shapes. We played all our old tapes and she held me without complaint as I drenched her nightdress; crying without end over another woman. She didn't try and ask me anything. But when Dusty's Breakfast in Bed came on, she said, "Who has hurt you again?" But I still didn't say anything.

Then

How could I say that surely it was not ***my*** Karin but this other Karin that had hurt me? It was this other one that suddenly threw her hands at me. That grabbed my breasts! That twisted my nipples until I cried out. And then held on, looking down at me through burning blue and white eye holes of a pale grey mask of a disfiguring fury.

The copier had stopped its run. Its motor began its tic tic as it cooled. I could hear tramping feet of normal school activity on the floorboards above. I heard the telephone ring and the doorbell before at last she let go. When I opened my mouth to speak, to explain, she shook her head at me like a dog or a wolf, her blond hair falling across the mask that quickly began to fade back into Karin.

I know there must be only one Karin. I know it ***was*** my Karin's angry slash of a mouth, so unusually acrid and sour that crushed me with words far more violent than her violent hands. It ***was*** Karin's lips that twisted and spat: "Us? There is no us! It was just a seedy affair in a car park!" It ***was*** Karin that grabbed at my photocopies and threw them at me. It ***was*** Karin that walked out as they hurled themselves against the wall and then fluttered to the floor covering my feet.

Now

Last week I brought back the box from my office drawer. I wanted to read all those letters. I wanted to try and make sense of what happened: to make sense of Karin, of me, of us. ***There was an us: I know there must have been some kind of us.***

Every night, as soon as Dian falls asleep (or pretends to sleep), I take out a letter or a story or a postcard and read it over and over. I still can't understand what any of them mean.

Why would she send me a rubber ring and a children's book about learning to swim. Where did she get that story about dangerous music and giant crushing stones? What angry gods? Why cracked jars and whose spilled flour? What's the meaning behind a half sentence, a half confidence?

What was she trying to say to me? Did she expect me to know? Why did she only ever speak to me in cartoons or by green writing? Why do I find them so condemning, so disturbing?

Grace would know. But I can't show them to Grace. She would not like these letters. She would have no patience with them nor would Dian. Nor Erica, nor Marie, or anyone I know and now I've let it in again, nor my "private mind".

Where does abuse begin and end? Does it only begin with a physical act and end when the pale purple bruises fade and the skin forgets? Does abuse start with persuasive sexual coercion disguised as a passionate love?

Can abuse be incremental drips of rejection; a switch on, switch off affair? Should a constant deluge of incomprehensible writings full of hinted awfulness even be called abuse? Is abuse implied criticisms and clever covert intimidation? Can "horse play" just get out of hand? Can that – what happened ***then*** – what can that be called – if not abuse?

With every word I write my "private mind" assures me that ***all of it*** is abuse. ***And that us was never love. It was so much less than love!***

CHAPTER SIX

Lecce

The working day for Lecce had settled into a gut-churning pattern. She would walk the distance from Dian's to their building and take the back entrance. There she would hesitate, surreptitiously scanning the car park. The absence of smoked darkened windows incongruously set into a small grey car meant, almost certainly anyway, that Karin had failed to turn up again. Then she would begin to relax, the frantic bird-like flutter in her stomach would ease and she would put on her "game" face.

As she crossed the grassy area and made for the steps, she reflected on the irony of being relieved when a member of the teaching staff failed to materialise. Guiltily she added the days – this would be the second Wednesday of absence. Two weeks and two days since Karin had … As always, her thoughts would swerve determinedly away from completing the sentence. If she refused to think about it, if Karin never came back, when the bruises completely faded, perhaps she could just carry on her life as if they had never met?

Here, in this untidy hectic environment, it was easy to rush through the day. In the time she now thought of as ***before,*** she would long for a quiet moment alone or to just sit down and have a quick coffee with Marie. Now she actively pursued one task after another, brushing aside any fleeting thought that threatened to impinge on all her frenetic activities that would send her spiralling down into the abyss.

The evenings were more difficult. Contemplating having to stop work and leave always sent her spirits plummeting. She could not bring herself to go back to her own apartment. There she would creep from room to room, from window to window, peering through the curtains onto the empty road, panicking when the phone rang and fending off her parents. As long as she could stay with Dian, who never questioned her restless pacing through to the early hours, she could cope. It was better not to sleep. Sleep meant more nightmares or half-waking vivid flashbacks of a pale face transfigured by violence and angry hands reaching out to hurt her.

She felt her insides begin to tremble again but this was just the start of the day. Jenny and Rose could be glimpsed through the opened blinds of the window. Lecce waved and hurried through the back door. Perhaps she could help out with the morning rush. There was something soothing in the way those two could interact so wordlessly together. Nothing prevented them from getting all their daily routine done, whatever havoc whirled about them. She knew that being with them was helping her hide but right now she needed to let their unsuspecting united calm wash over her for a while.

The irritating small nervy flutter returned as soon as she reached reception. There was something in the way the two greeted her that caused Lecce, with her heightened senses already on overdrive, to sense the strain in their smile and the quick covert glance they exchanged. Jenny half turned, putting the post back onto the desk and out of sight.

"She's in," Rose stated flatly, not bothering to hide her dismay as she raised one immaculate eyebrow towards the ceiling.

There was a brief embarrassed pause and even the noise from the corridor just outside seemed to drop away. Another look passed between the two women as Jenny's hand slowly came from behind the counter and with an air of apology, she held out a slim purple envelope.

"She left this for you before she went upstairs."

It was obvious to Lecce that any pretence was unnecessary. There was no point in asking "Who?" Somehow that certain knowledge came as a relief. Their faces were showing only concern and not the judgement she had long imagined. It was that, rather than the rampaging anxiety beginning to take hold, that brought tears to her eyes.

Impulsively, she moved behind the counter and gave Jenny a quick hug and said with a tight smile,

"Don't look so worried, Jen. I'm not going to shoot the messenger!" and with shaking fingers pried the letter out of her protective grip.

"Don't read it, New Boss. It will bring you nothing but bad!" Rose stabbed a crimson nail at the battered machine in the corner, already piled high with old documents and exam papers. "I'll shred it for you."

"It's a tempting thought, Rose." Lecce gave an unhappy laugh, picturing the shredder's jagged teeth biting into the ominous coloured missive. It would end up as nothing more than a dozen purple ribbons that could conveniently disappear into the bin.

"But I have to read it." Lecce swallowed the painful realisation that Karin never did anything by accident or on impulse. "Not now though. I can get to my mail later today," she said, replacing the letter on her tray, quickly covering it with the remainder of her post.

★★★

Throughout the soporific routine of reception, flanked by her friends, Lecce had drifted in and out of a comforting state of wellbeing. For five or ten minutes at a time, her threaded nerves would forget the brooding presence above her head and cease listening for that distinctive step on the wooden staircase or across the gravel leading to the car park.

By three thirty, with the last footfall and the final swing of the back exit, she was growing convinced that Karin must have left by the front door. At four o'clock, she was almost certain that delivering the letter must have been the sole intent. That they had once again entered into their unspoken pact of mutual avoidance.

Rose had gone off with Marie on one of their paper trail errands half an hour ago. Jenny was still trying to extricate herself from a telephone query that had begun ten minutes earlier as Lecce pulled aside a few of the slatted blinds. Sighing, she reached across to the wall cabinet for the spare set of keys, disappointed not to see the reassuring sight of Billy's bicycle chained to the railings. It was way past time for the upstairs lock up and so the job would fall on her.

Although there was still nearly an hour to go before dusk, the cold night had come early and there was only a subdued blue glow from emergency lighting reflecting off the cream paint and onto the stairs. She rushed through each floor, belatedly thinking of the torch Billy always took with him. As she eagerly began to turn the final latch, a thin shadow, spookily exaggerated across the upper half of the wall and onto the ceiling, made a sudden appearance.

Lecce stifled an involuntary scream and grabbed at the banister as the shade, gliding its way up the few steps to join her, lost its ghostly shape and materialised into its human form.

"Dear me!" Karin's lips were a thin sarcastic line. "Did I give you a fright Ms Connor?"

"Was there something you wanted from upstairs?" Lecce forced a response, fighting the urge to lean further away into the wooden handrail.

"Well, I wanted you," Karin whispered as she moved another step forward, dipping her head down, until their lips were almost touching. "I mean I wanted to see if you had read my note, that's all ... unless you ..." she trailed off, stepping away, adding with a low harsh laugh, "No, of course not. I don't want that, but I bet you still do."

"I haven't got to my post yet, Karin." Lecce helplessly flushed at the casual insult. "But if it's not about work then I don't think we should be exchanging letters anymore. I think we should just ..."

"Look! It is about work. Well, sort of anyway. So just run along and read it!"

In the grey light Lecce watched Karin's features grow still and hard, irritation beginning to cloud her eyes. She saw, thought she saw, those long slim hard hands reach out towards her.

"Don't touch me!" The half-healed bruises seemed to throb and sting, her mind flooding with a kaleidoscope of panicky images. Without conscious thought, she raised her own hands and with flat palms pushed hard against Karin's chest.

Karin stumbled down half a step, yelping out her surprise as she gripped the railing to stop her fall. Briefly, their eyes met in stunned disbelief until Karin's slid away to the floor and Lecce heard herself say, as if from a long, long distance,

"Karin. I promise. I will read your note. But I think you should go home now."

"Alright, I will." Karin's foot absently scrapped against the final step as another potent silence grew. Lecce just had time to register something approaching regret or maybe despair on the younger woman's face before it settled back into its habitual, cool, unreadable pose.

For a second Karin seemed as if she was searching for something more to say then roughly pulled aside the neck of her sweater. She tugged at a delicate chain around her neck until it snapped. The broken necklace dangled momentarily across her fingers and then travelled upwards as she tossed it towards Lecce with a casual sweep of her arm.

"I'm my own guardian angel. I can look after myself," she muttered, her words just reaching Lecce who had remained quite still, her hand clutching at the rail, heart racing and ashen faced with shock. Had she really pushed Karin? Had she wanted to hurt her or just protect herself?

As Karin retreated down the remaining steps and swung through the back door, a cold draught of winter air rose up the staircase. Lecce shivered and absently stopped to pick up the fallen necklace, dropping it into her jacket pocket.

She slowly lowered herself down onto the top step, waiting patiently for her tangled nerves to calm. In the quiet she could hear Karin's fading footsteps, her own erratic heartbeat, feel the rush of blood through her pulse and a potent mixture of loss and relief flood through her.

Her fingers turned over the small hard object in her pocket. How much love had gone into the giving of that gift, of the giving of self? How little, how much less, she had been given in return. Was it time to become her guardian angel too?

CHAPTER SEVEN

Lecce, Erica, Marie

Lecce had made a point of picking up her mail first thing the following morning but then stopped irresolutely at the top of the basement stairs, fighting the urge not to rush outside and back to the safety of the open road. Finally, she made a careful descent, catching herself counting under her breath in the way the children from the crèche often did, right down to the fourteenth and final step.

For such a large, sprawling building, there never seemed to be any hiding place. She could tell by the filtered light from the gaps beneath the door and from muted voices that drifted into the hallway that their office was already occupied. There was laughter and the clinking of cups coming from the staff room. She flung the pile of mail onto the bottom step whilst she frantically searched her jacket. The only other rooms led to the cleaner's cupboard and the toilets. As she picked out the right key she hesitated, despair and self-loathing almost making her choke. Was she really going to cower in the cleaner's cupboard before she could bring herself to open the letter or worse, hide in a Ladies' cubicle?

With unintended vigour, Lecce pushed open the door and with no more than a muted "Good morning", made straight for her desk and immediately began tearing at her post. Oblivious to the puzzled astonishment that registered on the faces of Erica and Marie, her own remained composed, as if she was completely absorbed in her task. With sightless eyes, she blindly placed one piece of correspondence after another on her in tray. Her mind feverishly contemplated the possible contents of the only piece of correspondence that really mattered.

It was impossible not to remember when a letter on the mat or a note from Karin waiting for her in the morning had been something that had painted her day wonderful. In the beginning, there had been an avalanche of charming compliments, poems and funny cartoons all scribbled in an almost unreadable hand. As she considered the familiar green spidery script that spelt her name, holding it between thumb and forefinger, there was a sudden treacherous desire to forgive and excuse: to forgive the unforgiveable, excuse the inexcusable.

For some time, Lecce was completely unaware of the way Erica and Marie's conversation had quickly become forced and desultory; a hushed passing back and forth of workbooks and sheets of statistics. That the room had fallen silent slowly penetrated even her mind's wild clamour. With a sinking feeling of defeat, she gave up on her deception and faced their questioning gaze. She looked from one friend to another, unconsciously straightening her shoulders, before deliberately tearing open the purple envelope.

The headline, from the roughly cut newspaper, hit her like a sharp smack between the eyes. Flushing a deep crimson before turning a sickly pallid grey, she instinctively jerked back and away from the newsprint. Whatever it was she had expected, had feared or hoped for, it was not this.

Baffled, she read and reread the headline: "Deputy Head faces Tribunal for Sexual Harassment." Is this what Karin truly believed had been between ***them?*** She hardly bothered to do more than scan the article. The kind of salacious tale it would tell was obvious. The accompanying note consisted of two capitalised sentences: "I've joined a union, just so you know." And "I probably need counselling now." Is this how she intended to "look after herself first"?

Lecce hesitated, crumpling the paper in her hands, all thoughts of excuses and forgiveness evaporating under a deluge of indignation which was quickly replaced by the sobering recollection of the near accident on those treacherous stairs. Keeping her mouth shut was no longer an option.

"I have been so unbelievably stupid," Lecce said finally, tentatively, as if testing to see if she still had a voice. She studied her colleagues through a blur of contrite tears as Marie, looking horrified, half-rose from her chair and Erica, her face impassive, betrayed her anxiety by smoothing her skirt over her knees.

"But not this!" she blurted. "What I've done is bad enough but ***that*** is a thing I hope you know I would never do!"

Marie swiftly crossed the room and plucked the article from Lecce's still twisting fingers. Taking it to the window, she smoothed open the page and let the low light fall onto the cramped messy newsprint. Under her breath, lips framing each word, she read the whole commentary twice over before fiercely shaking it as if sheer force could cause the words to slip from the page and disappear through the floorboards.

"How dare she threaten you like this? It's just bloody ridiculous!" Marie angrily flattened the pages with her palm and gave them to Erica. "I'm sorry, Erica, but this is too, too much!"

"Don't bother to apologise, Marie," Erica said whilst she scrabbled for her glasses somewhere beneath the litter that was her desk. She barely glanced at the newspaper, before adding dryly, "Of course it's bloody ridiculous!"

Their manager sighed inwardly. It was all too sad and sordid and so avoidable. "But Lecce, surely it was obvious that the girl is unreliable and troubled?" A flash of irritation, compelling her to add, "What on earth were you thinking?"

Lecce shook her head, staring blankly down at the desk, making no effort to stem the tears dripping onto the envelope. What had she been thinking? Had she been thinking at all? What kind of blind Cupid had dulled all her common sense? Why had it taken actual physical violence before she had known how to step away?

"Well, never mind, what's done is done." Lecce's stricken face and Marie's look of reproach prompted Erica to soften her words. "Nothing will come of it," she said, with an air of finality, whilst at the same time deftly slipping the envelope and its contents inside an already open manila file.

As if to emphasise her words, Erica closed the folder and put it into her top drawer, shutting it away with a dismissive snap.

"Now," she said dryly, smoothing her skirt and rolling her chair away from the desk, "Let's have a cup of tea and then I suggest we just get on with business as usual."

Picking up her thick appointments diary, she handed it to Lecce, saying in a brisk tone that would brook no argument, "I suggest you deputise for me at these meetings for the rest of today and tomorrow. And Marie, perhaps you will cover anything that needs doing for Lecce until Friday."

★★★

"Are you going to be alright?" Marie inspected Lecce anxiously as they stood together at the exit. Lecce was still a deathly pale and shivering as much from shock as from the bright but raw, winter's morning.

"Here," Marie took off her own scarf and wound it round her friend's neck and pulled up the half-open zipper of her jacket. "You need to keep warm if you're going to get to all those meetings!"

Lecce gave a ghost of a wry smile and weighed the diary Erica had given her in both hands. "Erica's made sure I'll have travelled the length and breadth of the capital before I'm done!"

Despite the awfulness of the morning, a brief amused look passed between them, as they pictured the way their boss had so decisively diffused the situation, making them drink tea before sending them both packing.

"She was rather magnificent wasn't she?" said Marie.

"You both were." Lecce squeezed her arm and then added, thinking of Jenny and Rose from the day before, "You all were; you all are."

★★★

Lecce hurried away from the building and from Karin, whose tall shadow she had glimpsed half hidden by the window blind on the first floor. Head bent, she made her way down the leafless wind-chilled avenue, tucking herself further into the comfort of Marie's scarf, touched and grateful for its protection.

With every step, a faint shaky sense that something had imperceptibly shifted for the better took hold. Was it possible that speaking up had weakened whatever sick thing had struck at her heart? Was its grip only ever as strong as her silence?

Waiting at the crossing for the green light, she resolved to face whatever came next. Somehow, she would find the voice she had lost. She would try and take care of their precious department first and then, if it was possible, herself.

And when it was over, she would pack it all away and never think of it, never speak of it again.

CHAPTER EIGHT

Erica and Karin

Erica watched the two as they progressed across the cluttered car park until she saw them pause at the exit. Then she waited a full five minutes before reopening the drawer and taking out the file. This time she studiously read through the article and considered all its possible implications, her lips pulling together in distaste.

Lecce had indeed been foolish to involve herself with such a manipulative little so and so. Yet ***she*** had put off talking to her, time and time again. Procrastination never did anything, or anyone, any good. At the very least, she should have done more than just call on Dian and hope it would all go away. With a sharp stab of remorse, she acknowledged that she had found the excuse of minding her own business very convenient.

Throwing off her glasses, her gaze returned to the barred and grubby window. She could just glimpse the stark shapely charm of the slender silver birch and the rare brilliant blue of a January sky. She pushed aside the offensive document and schooled her eyes and thoughts to focus only on the surprising beauty of their urban landscape. She listened for a while to the blackbird and the robin's chatter. Amused, she observed an early squirrel caper across the ivy-clad wall as it made for the peanuts Jenny or Rose always left for them.

Once her usual pragmatic calm was restored, Erica replaced the envelope and then reluctantly unclipped a photocopy from Karin's details. As she deliberated, her fingers creasing and re-creasing the fold, her mind returned to her unexpected fraught exchange with Dian on Tuesday. At the time she had attempted to argue the ethics of looking at something so personal without Lecce's permission, and of making an actual copy to pass on to a third party until her companion had uncharacteristically snapped:

"Oh, come on, Erica! This is more than a matter of ethics," she had said with unaccustomed vehemence. "We can indulge in an ethical discussion some other time. Believe me, I would not have read this, I would never ask you to sully your precious conscience, unless I thought it was unavoidable!"

She, if not Dian, who was agitatedly waving the paper about as if swatting a fly, had become aware of suspended teacups and the curious scrutiny from nearby tables. She hurriedly stuffed the copy into her bag, vaguely promising to think about it later. Pursuing her advantage, Dian had then pressed a few letters on her saying, "You don't have to read these, but you might need them. You know, just in case you have to show your hand."

Erica, of course, did not "know", but had taken them anyway vainly hoping that everything would remain untouched and eventually forgotten inside the growing file entitled Karin Pedersen.

Resigned and smothering any remaining flicker of uncertainty, Erica opened the copy and struggled to decipher the cramped and frantic diary entry that began, "How could I say that it was my Karin ..."

★★★

Karin had sent her students off early and was waiting with a growing unease. She had begun today fairly confident that Lecce would have come to her senses. But it was late for a Friday afternoon, and now she was not so sure.

Karin brooded over that touching little scene she had observed between Lecce and Marie yesterday morning. Marie had definitely been doing the mother hen routine, what with all that scarf winding and jacket fastening! Since then, there had been no sign of Lecce anywhere in the building. Those witches in reception had clammed up when she had asked them where she was: she had not liked the way they had looked at her either.

She continued to complete page upon page of the endless job applications Jack had practically flung at her when he had eventually turned up on Tuesday evening. It was leave the college or leave the house, he had insisted. Had he meant it? She thought of his pale tired face and the unfamiliar coldness in his eyes and of the bloody bandage still roughly wrapped around his hand. She relived the silence of those empty long days and the even longer nightmarish nights alone in the house and decided that this time, he had.

Karin bit at her lip and shook herself free of that thought. She would win him over, she always did. Why had she ever thought it might be fun and safe to indulge in a little conquest with a woman? It was over now, and all Lecce had to do was keep quiet and write references, so where was she?

The rush and excitement of leaving students had faded from the building, along with any remaining daylight and there was still no sound of footsteps making their way to her door. With an effort, Karin stopped herself picking at the already weeping sores around her nails and gave up the wait. Lecce was not coming, not now, probably not ever.

She began an exasperated shove of her belongings into her bag, fighting back waves of panic. For once her head was full of disjointed thoughts and a dim recognition that her own actions had got her into this mess. That article was not such a good idea after all. It was those green pens. Once she got them out, everything always spiralled out of control. Why did Jack always sit back and let it happen? Why hadn't he stopped her for once?

★★★

Erica paused and with an overdue caution, brought her hand quickly back to her side. She told herself that it was hardly likely that ***she*** had anything to fear from this enigmatic sylphlike creature just a mere few feet away on the far side of the door. Yet that harrowing account of the sudden act of violence against Lecce was here in the file, along with a clumsy attempt at blackmail. In a purple prose envelope of all things!

Perhaps she should have told Marie where she was going or have waited until Billy did his floor check. But it would be better for everybody, including Karin, if she could put an end to this insanity quickly and quietly, with the least possible fuss.

She took a deep breath and gave it a few more seconds, reassured by at least having the element of surprise on her side. She gave a light yet determined rap at the door and carefully rearranged her lips into the thin professional line her last course had advised for managing difficult people. "Difficult" did not come close to describing Karin Pedersen. But it would have to do.

"I just thought I'd come and say hello," she said, briskly making her way in, the knock only half complete. Was her tone at least approximating the cool but friendly one she had practised on her way up? Pulling across a stray chair, she sat opposite, determinedly ignoring the flash of irritation that Karin hardly bothered to conceal.

"I'm just about to go home." Karin finished packing her bag and then half turned, shrugging first one arm into her jacket and then the other, painstakingly placing each button through its hole without a glance at the other woman.

"I shan't keep you long. Are you quite recovered?" Erica pressed on, holding her pleasant expression, anticipating that Karin would eventually have to engage in some kind of dialogue.

She settled into her chair and prepared for the inevitable deadlocked silence, taking the opportunity for a surreptitious look at the girl opposite. There was still a faint flush of annoyance creeping across the cheekbones of the otherwise enigmatic and bloodless face. From the corner of her eye, Erica observed the tight fist clutching the handle of a battered briefcase at her side and the foot that twisted and ground at the floor beneath the desk.

During their stalemate she gradually became aware of the unusual bleak appearance of the room. No attempt had been made to hide the failing plaster or the grubby handprints with cheerful posters. The notice board was bereft of student work or photographs. An unreported damaged plug socket dangled and a broken sash cord had been carelessly tied into a grubby knot. As old as the building was, she was sure she had never encountered such an unloved room. Was there something in its forlorn aspect that somehow seemed to reflect back onto its occupant?

An unexpected flash of empathy floated briefly across her mind. Who or what had blighted this obviously clever and good-looking young woman's life? Sternly, Erica reminded herself of the reason for being here. She deliberately recalled the appalling assault and the needless cruelty and the threat of the news cutting. She considered the danger to her colleague and to her beloved department's reputation, hardened her heart and waited for a reply.

As the silence lengthened, Karin also considered the other woman through veiled lids and speculated on the real reason for this visit. As if Erica would give a toss about the state of her health!

"As I said, I was just about to go home," she replied cautiously, lifting her hand from her bag and examining her watch with an exaggerated care.

"Shall we make an appointment for Monday instead?" Erica hurriedly opened her file and selected a sheaf of neatly stapled statistics, and held them out adding, "Without meaning to pry, I did think that perhaps you must have an ongoing health issue which is causing you to take so much time off."

Karin started and stared at the pages blankly, her mouth dropping open before clamping shut. There can't have been that many. The stupid fussy old woman must have made a mistake in her sums! Shrugging, she leant back on her chair until it balanced on its two back legs.

Erica dropped the papers onto the table, pushing them towards her with a careful politeness. "Perhaps you might prefer to meet with one of our Occupational Health team to discuss anything of a more …" she hesitated delicately," … personal nature?"

"No, thank you. That isn't necessary." Karin began to pick at a nail. She stuffed both hands into her pockets, her eyes fixated on the document.

Erica quashed an inconvenient compulsion to be kind. Instead she reached into the folder taking out a long, printed list of names and placed it firmly on top of the others. "These examination results were disappointing, don't you think?" she said gently.

Karin suddenly lifted her head and sat up, sweeping the papers into her open desk drawer before giving Erica a swift look of undisguised hatred.

"Students don't work hard. They fail exams!" She half stood, her voice raised and trembling.

"That's hardly my fault and you know what, Erica? I'm beginning to feel intimidated and I don't like to be intimidated."

"Oh dear, I'm so sorry, that was certainly not my intention," Erica said quickly with a small, apologetic smile. "Why not ask

Jack to come along with you if that would make you feel more comfortable?" she paused, with an afterthought she could not resist, "Or your union rep?"

Their eyes met briefly. Momentarily defeated, Karin slouched back down.

"Wednesday then – but I don't need anyone else!"

The older woman began to rummage around in the file. Karin's lips began to curl in sardonic amusement as Erica untidily emptied the folder's contents onto the table, probably searching for a pen. What a fuss she was making. The woman was ridiculous, she can't even organise a file for God's sake! Karin began to feel back in control. There was nothing she needed to worry about after all. Relaxing, she began to plan a way to evade Wednesday.

"Would Wednesday at 12.30 suit you?" Erica leafed through a couple of pages. Karin's eyes were drawn to the debris of scattered paperwork cluttering the desk. Even from this distance and although it was folded and upside down, the almost transparent nature of cheap paper betrayed a well-known hand. There was a corner of a purple envelope just visible beneath it and also the tips of several other recognisable colours from her envelope collection.

Without warning Karin noisily left her seat, savagely thrusting it aside. For a second they both tracked its progress as it took flight, slamming against the wall where it appeared to hover in suspended animation before toppling sideways onto the floor.

"You're obviously in a hurry." Erica gave the fallen chair another cursory glance, and then continued, as if nothing much out of the ordinary had happened, "So, I'll just write in 12.30, shall I?"

"No!" Karin stood at her full height, giving the impression of being far taller than Erica remembered. There was a barely suppressed volcanic anger that bristled and sparked and brought back the vivid description from the diary.

"No?" Erica echoed calmly, brushing her skirt with the back of her hand. "Which other day would suit?"

"No! Don't let's bother with this pantomime!" Karin's neck began a slow rare dark flush of heat. She would have to get out before she lost control; before that black void opened and swallowed her down.

She tore open her bag and pulled up the half-completed application forms, "I was planning to leave anyway. Let's call this a resignation meeting and then I can get away from here!"

"This is a surprise." Erica, with an effort had remained seated and had brought her hands to rest quietly in her lap. "Surely, we should talk this through. A resignation is a bit hasty isn't it?"

"I'll put it in writing, if you like." Karin wrenched at the open desk drawer and grabbed at an A4 pad.

"Well, if that's what you really want to do." Erica slid her pen across the desk. "But I would hate to think that I, or anyone else for that matter, may have upset you."

Erica studied Karin, who had dragged the seat upright and flung herself back down. Was there just a trace of childlike fear and distress beneath all the violent bluster? As they regarded each other, her own brown eyes were sympathetic but dogged as they tried to engage with the blue-grey of Karin's before she had dropped them to the table and picked up the pen.

"No one has upset me." Karin carefully enunciated each word, and scribbled a few rapid lines across the page before adding her signature with a heavy flourish.

Erica detected the faint trace of an accent, only just recalling that Karin was far from her own home, from family and friends, and felt again an inexplicable pity. How was this tempestuous young woman going to manage her life? Was there anyone who could truly help her? Was she mad, bad, or just too dangerous to know? She was most certainly beyond the kind of help they had to offer. Her priority had to be the health and well being of her students and staff. She was their guardian and must look after them first and foremost.

"I'll waive the usual week's notice," Erica said with all the firmness she could muster. "It's time I let you go home. Don't worry, we can send on your details."

★★★

Karin strode from the room, her bag swinging wildly and her head held high. Erica, though, was not unaware of the almost imperceptible droop of the shoulders as the girl disappeared through the open door. She listened to the wooden echo from feet taking two steps at a time and meticulously tidied her file, placing her pen carefully into its side pocket.

For a while she continued to sit, waiting until she caught the echo of the back door being pushed open and then flung shut on its rusty hinges. *Had she* sullied her "precious conscience"? Did the end ever justify the means? Well, some might say that Karin had been given – what was it called – a free pass. In which case it was to be hoped that she would learn from this, or at least have sense enough keep it away from her workplace in future.

Her thoughts then turned to Lecce. She had not been given a free pass. Perhaps it was better not to know what other unspeakable hurts she may have endured at the hands of the most unlikely of culprits. Probably Lecce would never truly break her silence. But she would mend. This place would help her mend. They would all help her mend.

Erica gave her skirt a final tug and gathered the papers from the drawer and her other things together, concluding that if nothing else, one thing was clear: whatever sad tragedy had recently played out between the walls of their old, almost ruin of a building, it had most definitely gone home with Karin Pedersen.

Making her own much slower progress down the three flights, she took a mental inventory of the room she had left behind. There must be enough money for a complete redecoration. In fact, perhaps it was time to give the whole house a long overdue spring clean.

End of Part Three

Epilogue

"Where you find truth Is where you find your reflection ...
Is where you find love"
Reflections of Truth, Suzy Kaseem

Present Day
Lecce

This February was a far cry from the last. Lecce looked through the clear shining plates of the greenhouse windows and up at the weak sun, set in an extraordinary cloud-free, azure sky. The smoke from the new bin's chimney was a pleasing long, thin, grey-black spiral, undisturbed by rain or cruel north-east winds.

She made herself comfortable in a canvas armchair and covered her knees with a rag of a blanket which still held onto the faint aroma of dog and summer damp grass. The bin could no longer honestly be described as "new". This past year had already discoloured its once proud gleaming metal sides with the familiar rust-red of the old one. But the chimney lid was true and the legs sound, and it was doing a good job.

Lecce bent down and reached under the bench dragging the box forward, whilst still keeping a careful eye on the fire that raged outside. There were still a few remnants waiting to be consigned to the flames: a half dozen letters in their distinctive coloured sleeves and last of all, the diary.

She pushed that aside and picked up the envelopes, holding them gingerly in both hands. Those disarming cheery hues certainly camouflaged the weight of the words hidden within. It would be good to see them go. These were not the early, charming jokey ones, jam packed with silly drawings, sexual innuendo and flattery. These bulky tomes, every page carefully numbered, were a bludgeoning litany of critical judgements and piercingly unfavourable comparisons – with Jack, with other managers, and finally with all other human beings!

The library had been a really useful source of information. Now, twenty years too late, she easily recognised the tell-tale hallmarks of a narcissistic "love-bomber"! Whether the letters had been flattering or furious it was all the same. They had been designed to conquer, to demean and, finally to destroy every atom of her self-worth.

Their poison had lain dormant and lethal in the shadows of her mind for far too long! Thrusting aside the blanket she made for the door, picking up her worn out goalkeeper's glove, a few extra sticks of kindling and the short iron poker. With a fierce movement she hooked off the lid and flung them inside the incinerator, pushing them down hard until they were completely engulfed and she was covered in a strangely cathartic thick blast of blackened smoke.

Vaguely triumphant, she went back in and straight away lifted the now insubstantial contents of the box onto the table. She carefully examined the familiar hard-backed jacket of the book she had once thought of as her "private mind".

The cover would have to come off although the dog-eared photographs stuck to it did not deserve to burn. Impatiently, she pulled until it gave way. As the innards snapped opened and fell, she was surprised by a sheaf of neatly stapled and paper-clipped pages which fluttered down and came to rest at her feet. Mid-bend, she paused, curious, but reluctant to investigate. Now was not the time for the box to deliver any more unwelcome truths.

Resolutely she began feeding the flames with page after page of the diary until very little was left. Why had she ever thought that all her reawakened memories would incinerate as easily as paper? Ignoring the scorching blast and the billows of smoke that stung her eyelids, Lecce peered down into the blazing inferno, searching for some kind of satisfaction, some kind of closure. There was a sudden glimpse of her final entry, curling and browning in the heat. Just before the page blackened and flaked and was gone she noticed with a tremor of shock that the corner had been turned down.

A slow burn of suspicion began to dawn as absently Lecce continued to fill the bin with broken twigs and small strips of kindling. What more than just the heat from the fire was causing her to feel so overheated and on edge?

The only person she knew that used to mark pages that way was Dian. It was one of those petty things they had often bickered over. She reached back into the box and picked up the paper-clipped sheets. Her heart lurched and thudded as she unfolded the photocopy and recognised her own frenzied handwriting and then sank as she discovered the slim purple envelope she had last seen in the hands of Erica.

With shaking fingers and a renewed sense of purpose, she threw them into the bin where the flames still licked greedily upwards. The lengthy sick leave stats and an attached list of examination details also went down to the fire. She added several more thin sticks of wood and a firelighter for good measure and spent a few minutes more poking and prodding and stirring the bottom of the bin thoughtfully until the heading on the sheets, ***Karin Pedersen,*** and all else, including the cardboard box, was dust and ashes.

Once she was certain that no stray spark of life lay hidden beneath the blackened mass, Lecce left her smouldering composter and returned to the greenhouse. For a full fifteen minutes she occupied her hands with filling the bird feeders, putting out water for any stray animals, covering her early broad beans and garlic bulbs with fleece and finally emptying her tea flask and hunting for a sandwich. Her mind, though, was frantically making connections: Dian – Erica – Marie and Rose.

Eventually she sat back down and covered her knees, restlessly playing with the folds of the soggy rough weave and carefully linked her thoughts together. She did not have to be a Miss Marple to work out that some of her carefully concealed secrets had been known for years by Dian and probably by the others. Without their interventions, how much further might she have spiralled down into that psychopathically induced vortex?

After today's findings, *all* her wilful amnesia was at an end. There was even a possible explanation for Karin's apparent impromptu resignation. Did it explain Erica's cryptic reply when handing her the scrappy few lines in answer to her hopeful: "Has she really gone?"

"Oh yes, she's gone … exit stage left, pursued by a bear!"

There had been a final note from Karin. It had burned with an incandescent kind of rage and she had immediately thrown it away. The ink was blue and was written in strange idiosyncratic English, full of unlikely misspellings from someone so literate.

"Your a despicable human beng. U an ur cronies are a waist of space. I shan't spend enymore time on U. Ever!!"

As this final, sad recollection slid back into her mind to join the others, Lecce waited expectant, prepared for the familiar pangs of hurt and pain to pierce her through to the marrow. Instead her mood lifted and she was filled with a sudden energy. An energy she had thought would be forever sapped by this long, year of painful introspection and by this afternoon's ritual burnings.

Lecce swiftly thrust the blanket aside and after a cursory check to make sure the fire was finally extinguished, she hurried to close up the greenhouse. The colourless pastel twilight would soon disappear and the long shadows would lengthen to envelop the whole of the narrow pathway. She would have to be quick or she would be caught inside the empty inky-black allotment. She reached the huge iron gate and snapped the lock just as absolute dusk fell and as the blackbird, prompted by the welcome street lighting, began its goodnight song.

She started on her walk home at a faster pace than usual. For once she was keen to be indoors. Her mind kept returning to the photographs she had rescued from her old diary. She pictured each image: the beach snap with Grace; their shared half-grown children and Ruby Red Dog. Her best-beloved Dad and her still very much alive Mum; both dressed in their finery at her long-ago graduation. The annual staff photo on the back steps of their ancient building, now demolished. It was easy to pick out Jenny from the statuesque Rose and the tall Marie in the back row, holding baby, Zoe. Erica, as always, centre stage, in her trademark over-long skirt and sensible shoes, the carefully coiffed hair as grey as her own was now! And of course, her precious, lost, Dian, in a stripy shirt, holding a bunch of bananas and grinning impishly at the camera.

She would carefully peel off the photographs from the cover and find somewhere she could display them. Could she make up a montage to hang on the wall, perhaps? She would call it her "true love gallery". Who cares if it's cheesy! Grace was good at arty things like that. She would have to ask her to help. And maybe, just maybe, she would somehow find the words to explain all these lost years.

Present Day

Awi

Awi had been unconvinced that an audience, made up chiefly of teens and twenties, would go for their kind of oldies hard rock gig. So far, though, there had been a good reaction and a lively queue had formed behind their sales table almost as soon as the first set had finished.

One box of discs had emptied and the other was half out. Just a few more customers and there would still be time for a nice cold beer. Awi's energy was sapped almost dry, was fading in the humid atmosphere. The only good thing about this Dive Bar was that people had to smoke outside and the windows were open!

Performing was no problem but without Linnea, they were taking turns doing everything else as well. Everyone was missing being organised by her. Awi was missing her most of all, not just for the roadie work and sales either. The hotel beds all seemed much harder and colder without her soft warmth and far too silent without her quiet night-breath. Sleep was slow to arrive now and even slower to shake off in the mornings.

The musician was taking money and handing over the albums almost on autopilot. A potent mix of tiredness, steamy recollections of Nea's soft skin and a glass of something cold fogging her thoughts. At last the final sale was done and Awi scrabbled in the cash tin for coins, barely glancing up, blindly handing them over before beginning to turn away.

"You know, I just love that song, 'Teetering on the Edge'."

Awi was startled by the maturity of a pleasant deep voice and by the pressure of long slender fingers as they collected the change. Mildly astonished, she stepped back from the counter and politely moved her hand away. Now at eye level, she saw that a tall woman, just into middle age, was looking across the merchandise and gifting her with an amazingly breathtaking smile.

She had a solidly trim figure, with a flawless creamy complexion. Her hair though, was a puzzling mismatch with the rest of her undeniably fine features. The cut was ultra short and sharp. It was coloured an unconvincing chestnut, although not an altogether unpleasing contrast against the pale blond of almost invisible brows and lashes.

"Reminds me of me, I suppose," the woman continued, with a small self-deprecating laugh, reaching across to pick up an events programme. Her light-blue eyes, assessing and cool, met the hazel of Awi's own, held onto them for a long moment before dropping back down to the handbill.

"You really like that one?" Awi fiddled self-consciously with her silver-grey plait, tossing it behind her shoulders, returning the smile, unable to suppress a small smug glow of satisfaction at the apparent interest from a very attractive younger woman. Was she coming on to her? It was unlikely, absurd even. There was a gold band on the wedding finger and besides, she was far too straight-looking.

"Yes, really!" the other woman repeated, her voice teasing, a hint of amusement lifting her full lips. "Underneath all of this I'm a hard rock fiend, like you! I've come straight from work. This is just my day disguise!"

"Sorry! I didn't mean that you wouldn't … that you were …" Awi hurried to amend the comment, horribly aware that uncannily, her private thoughts had been discerned.

"I mean, it's a rather full on technical kind of riff and not everyone likes it. People tell me the words are too hopeless!"

"Well, I love it." The woman appeared completely unfazed by Awi's embarrassed bluster and casually turned the flat packet over, trailing a finger down the title and credits.

"Awi Hansen. Is that you?"

"Yes, that's me." Awi gave an awkward grin, adding quickly, realising that the others were throwing meaningful looks and picking up their instruments, "I'm always teetering on the edge of saying something stupid!"

"It seems to me that we already have a lot in common, then. I'm Karin," she said in a mock whisper, slipping a folded note into the open cash box before sauntering away, elegantly pushing through the press of people.

Bemused, Awi watched the long graceful figure making its way back to the corner end of the bar where a much older man waited. He was sipping disconsolately at a cocktail, compulsively checking his watch and searching the crowds.

Intrigued and gratified, Awi glanced again at the note with an unfamiliar flutter of embarrassment, before slipping it into the sleeve of her guitar case. There had been many such notes over the years, although none had ever been written in green ink!

These days she never did more than trophy wave them at the others. But there was something about the mysterious alchemy of that smile. Something irresistible in the clever little cartoon of a bemused face with a speech bubble below the telephone number which asked, "Am I teetering on the edge of liking you?"

Should she call this woman, see what was behind the disguise? No, maybe not … probably …

The End

The author

Born in Kent in 1950 and now living in Wales, Carys Smith has already written several short stories and poems which have been widely published in anthologies both nationally and internationally. Before retiring, she worked as a teacher of English language and literature and later became one of a busy management team in various community education settings. She has also taught creative writing classes and continues to drop in and out of various local writing groups, sharing her own work and learning much from the work of others.
Carys loves sport, gardening and public speaking. A Little less than Love is her debut novel and she is currently writing the sequel.